MW00473706

Lone Star Sweetheart

Sweetheart Series · Book One

Shannon Sue Dunlap

Scrivenings
PRESS
Quench your thirst for story.
www.ScriveningsPress.com

For my ultimate dream supporters, Mom and Dad

Copyright © 2023 by Shannon Sue Dunlap

Published by Scrivenings Press LLC
15 Lucky Lane
Morrilton, Arkansas 72110
https://ScriveningsPress.com

Printed in the United States of America

All rights reserved. No part of this publication may be reproduced, stored in a retrieval system, or transmitted in any form or by any means—for example, electronic, photocopy, and recording— without the prior written permission of the publisher. The only exception is brief quotations in printed reviews.

Paperback ISBN 978-1-64917-286-0

eBook ISBN 978-1-64917-287-7

Editors: Regina Merrick and Linda Fulkerson

Cover design by Shannon Sue Dunlap and Linda Fulkerson - www.bookmarketinggraphics.com

This is a work of fiction. Unless otherwise indicated, all names, characters, businesses, events, and incidents are either the product of the author's imagination or used in a fictitious manner. Any resemblance to actual persons, living or dead, or actual events is purely coincidental.

How could she survive the night without a cookie?

Katherine Bruno pulled her hair into a slapdash ponytail and eyed the empty snack table with disgust. The only redeeming feature of Sweetheart's monthly town meetings was the tantalizing assortment of homemade goodies she could dunk in her coffee.

Had someone forgotten to post the refreshment signup sheet? The community center's faux-wood panel walls closed in on her at the thought. If this wasn't the best place to drum up support for pet adoption, she would duck out the back way.

The animal shelter needed foster families. She'd planned to write an article for her job at *The Sweetheart Clarion*, but the editor fired her before she finished. Of course, he hadn't used such a negative term. He'd hemmed and hawed about flagging readership and online portals for five minutes until she asked him to cut to the chase. No sense dragging out the inevitable. It wasn't the first time she'd been fired, and, thanks to her uncontrollable tongue, it probably wouldn't be the last.

A cluster of men stood behind Katherine in assorted versions of plaid flannel and jeans. "It's indecent! How could a woman betray her own husband?"

What had put their sleeveless undershirts in a twist? She poured herself a steaming cup of java. Its heat seeped through the thin paper cup and warmed her fingers as she tried to ignore them.

"The mayor's wife has gone loco!" another outraged male proclaimed.

Katherine sighed. She needed a sugar fix. There wasn't even a pink packet of artificial sweetener to take the edge off the dark, pungent brew in her hand.

The incensed male chorus behind her grew louder.

"What makes Lanette Johnson think she can run the town of Sweetheart?"

Ah, the surprise second candidate in the mayoral race. She should have guessed. Katherine glared over her shoulder, but they didn't notice. The men were too busy casting judgmental looks at the mayor's wife as she walked past wearing a matching leopard print ensemble.

"Lanette was always bossing poor Harry around anyway. Does she have to try and take his job away on top of it?"

Their tongues clicked in unison. Katherine gagged, and not because of the over-roasted coffee.

"Gracious words," she muttered under her breath. "Remember. Gracious words, girl."

Easier said than done. She'd been a straight shooter all her life. Ready to tell it like it was. Until an unexpected conviction hit her one morning when she was reading the book of Proverbs. *Gracious words are a honeycomb, sweet to the soul and healing to the bones.*

Had her words ever brought healing to anyone? Doubtful. She wanted to be a honeycomb, but her blunt speech was more akin to apple cider vinegar.

Katherine had purposed then and there to change her ways. She'd made it a whole month without breaking her resolution. Granted, she'd been sick in bed seven of those days with the flu. But if the men in this town didn't find a different subject soon, she might be tempted to forget her pledge. The accomplishment of curbing her caustic remarks for four excruciating weeks was too groundbreaking to throw away.

Keep your mouth shut, even if it kills you.

She raised the cup to her lips and took a long, hard swig. The bitter liquid slid down her throat, burning a scorched path straight to her empty stomach. Leaning against the wall, she watched the men sputter worse than an old tractor.

Jud Watson finger-combed his sizeable salt-and-pepper beard. "She'd never get away with that if she was my woman. I wonder if he can sue her."

Katherine took another sip. Staying silent just might kill her.

"Sue her for what?" Willy Walker crossed his arms and rested them on a belly, which protruded over his king-sized silver belt buckle. "It's not against the law for a woman to run against her husband for mayor."

"But Lanette shouldn't treat poor Harry so awful. He's held the mayor's office for sixteen years. Why is she making waves?"

Katherine closed her eyes and rolled her lips inward. She inhaled the scent of her coffee like an aromatherapy candle. Frustration rumbled around her throat in an irritated growl.

Gracious words. Gracious words. Gracious—

Since when did a woman require permission from her husband to enter an election race? This wasn't the dark ages. If Lanette wanted to run for mayor, let her run for mayor. Katherine might not vote for her, but she certainly wouldn't stand in her way. Mayor Johnson could fight for his job, fair and square.

The men continued, blissfully unaware of how close they were to being verbally shish kebabbed. She squeezed her lids tighter as their clucking bounced against her ear drums.

"I heard Harry's hired some hotshot political consultant from New York."

"Lotta good that'll do him. What does a New Yorker know about Sweetheart, Texas?"

"Not much." A smooth, unfamiliar voice joined the discussion. "Do you mind filling me in?"

Katherine's lids popped open, and she observed the owner of the chocolate-textured baritone. Talk about honeycomb. This man's voice could sweeten her coffee for a year. Dressed in a tailored white button-down shirt and black dress pants, his lean frame stretched a head taller than the other men. Jet black hair combed in a professional side part. Dark eyes that sparkled—whether from amusement or disdain, she wasn't sure. And a serene expression showing no embarrassment at being gossiped about by strangers.

He drew a hand from the pocket of his slacks and held it out. "Let me introduce myself. Ryan Park. I prefer baseball over basketball. Eat way too much red meat and tend to be a little OCD about my office space. I'm the hotshot consultant. Although, I'm not sure I deserve the distinction. We'll see how good a job I do."

The men cleared their throats in an awkward chorus. Feet shuffled as they shook his hand, one by one, their gazes not quite meeting his.

"No offense meant," Willy mumbled as he tugged on his belt buckle.

"None taken." The newcomer waved away the apology. "I'd be curious too."

Curious couldn't begin to describe Katherine's emotions. She stared with her mouth open like a kid finding the deep-fried bubblegum stand at the state fair. Her feet moved forward without asking permission. She dashed to the group and stuck her hand out, the coffee cup still clasped in her other.

"Katherine Bruno." Since when had her voice been so breathless? "Welcome to Sweetheart, Mr. Park."

"My friends call me Ryan." His strong fingers wrapped around her own. "What do you prefer—Kathy, Katie, Kate?"

"I prefer Katherine. Thank you for asking."

Was this what romance novels meant by love at first sight?

She'd scoffed at the idea in the past, but her heart bounced like it was on a pogo stick. Any moment now, the angel choir would launch into song.

"Did you really come all the way from New York for our mayoral race?"

"Yes, ma'am."

She didn't relish being called ma'am. Katherine smoothed her messy ponytail at the nape of her neck. Perhaps she should have brushed her hair before the town meeting. But how was she to guess a gorgeous stranger would appear? Temporary retreat might be the best option. A quick dash to the restroom for damage control and a little lip gloss.

Katherine stepped away with reluctance. "I hope to see you around, Ryan."

"Count on it."

His easy smile warmed her from top to toes. She tottered a little as she turned. Had he meant anything in particular? Or was he being polite? Love at first sight could go both ways. Katherine paused to grab her gray messenger bag from a nearby chair.

Please, God. Let there be a comb in here.

Her hand still tingled where it had come in contact with her destiny. She shook her fingers, slipped her purse strap over her shoulder, and searched for a trash can to toss her cup.

Willy Walker's hearty voice boomed behind her. "Tell me, Mr. Park. Can you help our Harry-boy? His wife's a tough opponent."

"Please, call me Ryan. And trust me. I'm here to make sure the mayor's office stays blue instead of powder-puff pink."

Katherine side-eyed the group. The men guffawed, and she bit the inside of her cheek. She'd give him one pass. Think of what beautiful children they could make together.

"After all," he hooked his thumbs in his pockets, "there's a natural order to things. The mayor can run the town, and his wife can run the Ladies Auxiliary. Everybody wins."

Katherine's hand cooled. The five-second fantasy was nice

while it lasted. She took the last swig of her coffee, crushed the cup, and tossed it in a trash can. Who needed sugar?

She did a 180-degree turn and barged into the cluster of testosterone. "I doubt the mayor could've even found his blue office without his wife directing him all these years. *Mister* Park."

RYAN PARK'S inner warning bell rang. The last time he'd heard it was when his boss asked him to take the Sweetheart job as a personal favor. It seemed the mayor of this tiny burg was an old college buddy of hers, and she wanted to lend him the best on her roster. How could he argue? He had a perfect record: seven candidates, seven wins.

So here he was. Podunk, USA.

His goal was to make the small-town exile as quick and painless as possible. He'd do a bang-up job and avoid any obstacles, no matter what or who they might be. The steel spark in this lady's green eyes told him she was looking for trouble.

He hadn't meant for her to hear his chauvinistic comment. It was crafted for the good ol' boy's network around him. The last thing he needed was an angry feminist on his case. Time to smooth some ruffled feathers. What was her name again?

"Katherine." It was a fact people responded to the sound of their own name, and he used his most conciliatory tone as he said it. "I apologize if I offended you. I didn't mean anything derogatory against Mrs. Johnson. I understand she's a wonderful woman."

The tall brunette who reached almost to his nose snorted. "Lanette is bossy, opinionated, and entirely too fond of creating new projects and recruiting others to do the dirty work."

Ryan hesitated. Was she defending the mayor's wife or not? "I don't—"

"But she's also the driving force keeping this town afloat.

With her help, Sweetheart got out of the red for the first time in decades. She built our annual Candy Hearts Festival from a backwater, one fire engine parade into a well-advertised celebration that tourists from around the state come to enjoy. The event's revenue makes up half of our yearly budget." Katherine glared at the men around her. "Yes, she's pushy as all get out, but at least she moves us in the right direction."

"Now, Katie," one of the plaid-covered gentlemen said. "He didn't mean anything by it."

She rounded on him. "And you didn't mean anything, Willy, when you called Lanette indecent?"

"I—we—we just got a little riled up." Willy retreated and raised his hands in front of him. "You of all people should relate."

"Harsh words may be my trademark, but at least I say them to your face." She stuck her chin out. "You won't find me tacking a gossip sign to someone's back while they're not looking."

Ryan's practiced smile sank into a more natural smirk. If there was one thing a political consultant valued and seldom received, it was honesty. He got the feeling he'd never have to wonder what this eloquent firecracker was thinking. Give her a microphone and a makeover, and he could run her for state senator. Time to employ his most tried-and-true strategy —flirtation.

"Katherine." He laid his hand behind her shoulder, too low to be impersonal, but not low enough to be considered harassment. Only enough to fluster her and make her lose her focus.

She whipped around—eyes wide.

"It's obvious how much you value Lanette." He lowered his voice and moved a centimeter closer. "Would you consider helping me? I was hoping to convince Mrs. Johnson to drop her campaign and support her husband's re-election. Their teamwork made Sweetheart the thriving place it is today, and she's an integral part of his success."

Was that a quiver under his fingers? He must be getting to her. This was going to be easier than he thought.

He turned his smile up a degree.

Her lips quirked in response. She leaned near enough her soft breath brushed his earlobe.

"This kind of trick may work in the big city, Mr. Park. But I was raised on my uncle's ranch. I recognize the smell of manure." She brushed him off and headed for the door.

The cluster of middle-aged gentlemen around him snickered. The one with the unnaturally large belt buckle slapped him on the back.

"Wooo-eee. You've only been in town a few hours, and you already met the sharp end of Katherine Bruno's temper. Did you get on the Almighty's bad side, son?"

"How do you mean?" Ryan watched the furious figure stomping away.

"You've heard of that story *The Taming of the Shrew*? Folks suspect Katie's father named her after the main character. She can slice the skin right off your heart with one lash of her tongue. 'Best beware her sting.'"

Ryan's eyebrows dipped.

A local quoting Shakespeare?

Add that to the potent set-down he'd received from the pretty shrew, and he might have to revise his campaign strategy for Sweetheart. Apparently, they weren't a bunch of gullible hicks he could sweet talk into following his lead. He slipped a hand in his pocket to grab a roll of antacids.

This was going to be harder than he thought.

Chapter Two

R yan tapped his clipboard against a shiny red fire hydrant as he scanned the main drag of Sweetheart. The blazing Texas sun glared on his head. He tugged the collar of his navy blue, Oxford shirt and fanned it from his neck.

High noon and nary a soul in sight. This job was supposed to be a restful change from the breakneck pace of New York City. But not this restful.

A feed-and-grain store, a Fifties-style diner, and an art gallery with a green-and-white striped awning stretched in front of him. The street was picturesque in that Christmas-television-movie kind of way. A well-manicured square with a statue of the town founder stood in the distance. It was the only figure in sight resembling a human being.

How was he supposed to take a benchmark poll without people? He popped an antacid in his mouth. The chalky substance dissolved under his teeth and sat on his tongue in a powdery film. Why didn't he bring a bottle of water?

The wind kicked up. An empty soda can rattled across the otherwise pristine road to where a sedan with a wicked dent in the door pulled to a stop. A woman sat behind the wheel.

Ryan made his way over as she climbed out. "Excuse me, ma'am."

She spun around with a glare. Oh, great! The touchy female from the community center. His stomach hollered for another antacid.

"Katherine, wasn't it?" He held up the clipboard and took a pen from his pocket. "I wonder if you could help me."

She slammed the door and crossed her arms over a black T-shirt with an Eighties rock band on the front. Her spine straightened, and her long, jean-encased legs braced against the pavement.

Time to ignore the resistant body language and plow ahead.

He pasted on his most endearing smile. "Since I'm new to Sweetheart, I need to get a feel for what people think. On a scale of one to ten, how would you rate Mayor Johnson's job performance over the past two years?"

"Should my score factor in the help his wife gave him?" Sarcasm dripped from her tone.

Ryan raised the clip on his board and trapped the pen underneath. "From what I hear, they make quite a team. It's a shame to split them up. Especially with the expansion plans the mayor has."

"Expansion plans?" Katherine uncrossed her arms. "I'm not sure what you mean."

Ryan smiled again. He'd caught her interest. Time to press his advantage.

"Mayor Johnson wants to announce it at his first official rally, but I can give you a little preview." He paused for dramatic effect. Might as well whet her appetite.

Her body tilted his way. "Preview of what?"

Ryan mirrored her posture. "The mayor lined all his ducks in a row before making it public knowledge. He's spent the last year and a half lobbying for funding from the governor, hiring architects, and picking out property. In twelve short months, Sweetheart will occupy a brand-new town hall."

The woman's mouth dropped. Oh, this was good. He'd won another vote for his client in a matter of seconds.

"A town hall?" Her gaze wandered to the side as she processed the information. "Won't that be expensive?"

"The mayor already arranged enough bonds to cover the cost. They can be paid off over a long period of time, and Sweetheart will enjoy a state-of-the-art facility with the latest computers, security, and—"

"How much?" Her eyes snapped to his.

"What?"

"How much money in bonds has he arranged?"

"The new building will house the sheriff's department, the town registrar, the mayor's office, and a meeting hall for the entire community. The expenses for construction and materials—"

"How. Much?" She spit the words from tightened lips.

Ryan hesitated. Without the architect's fancy renderings and projected drawings to sugar-coat it, the cost might seem high to a small-town girl.

"Fifteen million dollars, but the town will have thirty years to pay it off and—"

"Million?" She laughed. "Fifteen million dollars?"

"Trust me, ma'am—"

"Katherine." She jammed her hands on her hips. "And why should I trust you? This is your second day in town. I grew up in Sweetheart, and I know how long it took to drag this place out of the crippling debt the last mayor left it in. Now Harry Johnson wants to throw us right back in the hole?"

She stepped closer until his personal space was well and truly invaded. Was he imagining the heat exploding from her like a furnace? The belt buckle man at the meeting was correct. Someone hang a sign around this woman's neck.

Beware!

~

THE ANGRY WORDS rose in Katherine's throat and pricked at the roof of her mouth. Her lips ached to open and release every last poisoned dart in this pretentious man's face. Who was he to tell her what was best for her town?

Gracious words, Katherine. Gracious ... Lord, hit the censor button for me.

"Mr. Park—"

"Please, call me Ryan."

"No, thank you. Listen, Mr. Park, fifteen million dollars may be chicken feed in New York, but that amount is astronomical to the citizens of Sweetheart."

He tucked his clipboard under his arm and nodded. "I understand your concern. But the long-range benefits will far exceed the expense. Sweetheart needs a better place to hold town meetings than a dilapidated old community center, which hasn't been refurbished since Nixon was president."

"True, but—"

"And from what I understand, Mayor Johnson hasn't taken a salary once in the sixteen years he's held office. How could you doubt the intentions of such a man?"

"It's not his intentions I doubt, it's his intelli—"

Beep.

Katherine pulled her phone out. Was this God's subtle way of helping her keep her mouth shut?

She read the text, then looked at the handsome newcomer who waited with a patient but practiced smile.

"Excuse me, Mr. Park. I'm supposed to meet someone, and she's wondering where I am." Katherine gestured to the *Ma Cherie Salon* in the strip of stores beside them.

"No problem." He flourished a hand in the direction she indicated. "We can finish our discussion later. A good hairstylist is hard to find."

"It's not a—" She clamped her lips shut. Why did it matter what he thought? "Forget it."

Katherine held her head high as she stomped away and

yanked open the salon's thick mahogany door. The scent of jasmine invaded her nostrils. A row of empty massage chairs filled one wall, and sixty-eight-year-old Elise Walker sat at the manicurist's table with her silver-gray hair in rollers. Her high-pitched voice raised another octave when she spotted Katherine.

"You're here!"

"Hello, Elise. I got your text. What did you want?"

"It wasn't for me. Lanette! Come and see who walked through the door."

Lanette Johnson exited the side room in a purple terry cloth robe. A white piece of material flattened her short blonde bob and wrapped around her face, holding the sagging flesh up to her chin. She clapped twice as she approached Katherine.

"There's the girl I'm looking for."

Katherine recognized the militant gleam in the shorter woman's eyes. She'd spent the better part of her adult life avoiding Lanette's battle plans. The mayor's wife had two gears: full speed ahead and that's-not-fast-enough-kick-it-up-a-notch. The possibility of buying a ticket on her stressy-go-round made Katherine's blood pressure quiver.

She backed away. "Whatever new project you're cooking up, I don't have time."

"From what I hear," Lanette pulled at the tight, elastic band on her chin, "you have all the time in the world since the *Clarion* let you go."

Elise *tsk-tsked* from the manicure table. "So sorry, dear."

The small-town gossip mill was alive and well. News of her unemployment had probably traveled halfway to Dallas. The sudden craving for a chocolate chip cookie hit her.

"On the contrary." Katherine scooted another step. She wasn't above making a run for it if the persistent woman refused to take no for an answer. "Half the envelopes in my mailbox are bills. I'll be busier than ever hunting for a new job to pay them off."

"Then hunt no further." Lanette opened her arms wide. "I

witnessed your little clash with Harry's fancy political consultant last night. Those old buzzards think I'm deaf, but I heard them chewing me down as I walked by. Not that it mattered. I've got a particular reason for running for mayor, and I won't let a little gossip stop me."

"Good for you." Katherine resisted the urge to ask what Lanette's particular reason was. Better to know as little as possible, so she didn't get sucked into the whirlwind. "If you'll excuse—"

"Harry sent all the way to New York for Ryan Park, so he must be good. I admit it threw me for a loop when I found out. How was I going to compete with a professional? Then I heard you put him in his place as nice as you please," she raised her French-tipped fingertips heavenward, "and it hit me like the 'Hallelujah Chorus.' Katie, I realized you're perfect."

Perfect? Katherine savored the strange new compliment. People usually listed what she needed to fix about her prickly personality. Maybe she should hear this perceptive woman out.

"Perfect for what?"

"To help me beat my husband in this year's mayoral race. Katherine Bruno, I'm hiring you to be my campaign manager."

Static filled her brain. "Your what?"

"Whatever that Park guy is doing for my husband, you'll do for me. Get the word out. Drum up votes. You're a go-getter, Katie. If you're on my side, nobody can beat us. My husband will rue the day he scorned my advice."

"What do you mean, he—"

"Let's take a seat and plan our campaign strategy." The older lady grabbed her with the strength of a woman who had been bossing around an entire town for sixteen years.

Katherine's feet skidded against the tile floor. Why was Lanette wasting her time with crazy propositions?

"What do I know about politics?" She tried to shake her off —unsuccessfully.

"I don't need someone political. I need someone with grit.

Someone who won't melt in sympathy when my husband turns those big puppy dog eyes of his on them. You're smart enough not to fall for his homespun charms when he tries to talk you out of joining me."

"But, but I like Mayor Johnson."

"So do I." Lanette sank into the nearest recliner. "Liked him so much I married him." She wiggled her shoulders deeper into the leather cushions and hit the massage button. Buzzing sounded. Her body jiggled as the chair went to work. "But someone has to teach my man a lesson, and you're the gal to help me do it."

Katherine grabbed a piece of foil-wrapped chocolate from the candy bowl on the counter and sat on a sofa by the wall.

Lanette leaned forward, her polished fingernails clasped on her knees. "I wasn't kidding when I said I needed you, Katie. Sweetheart is in a whole heap of trouble if we don't do something."

"Trouble?" Katherine stopped unwrapping the candy.

"My husband got this idea in his head that we require a new town hall. The plan sounded good at first—until I saw the tab. He wants to spend—"

"Fifteen million dollars." Katherine's eyes rolled up under her lids.

Lanette's head tilted. "How'd you know?"

"A little birdie from New York told me."

"He's another unnecessary expense," she scoffed. "I love my husband dearly, but when it comes to money, he's a featherbrain. With my help, we've kept the town in the black for the past five years, but even I can't figure out a way to pay off fifteen million dollars. So, I decided to run for mayor. I don't desire the job, but someone has to stop Harry before he ruins us all."

It made sense. Lanette really didn't want to be mayor. And Katherine really didn't want to be her campaign manager. But did either of them really have a choice? She finished unwrapping the chocolate, popped it in her mouth, and sighed.

"Everyone thinks I'm a big-mouth troublemaker. How could I ever help you convince—"

"Whoa." Lanette pounded the chair button, and it stopped rocking. "Don't sell yourself short, honey. You were raised by your uncle, and we all remember what kind of man he was—mean as spit and driven by money. If you hadn't learned to holler, he would have forgot you existed."

Unexpected prickles hit Katherine's eyeballs. She blinked and looked away. Was it possible she could help save the town from another disastrous debt? Plus, she needed a way to pay next month's rent. She sighed again.

"Hang on, Lanette. I should speak to somebody first." She rose from her seat and headed for the exit.

"Wait, darlin'," Lanette called after her. "Are you going to help me?"

"Yes!" Katherine bellowed without turning around. She might be giving in, but she didn't have to be happy about it.

She swung open the heavy wooden door and squinted in the sunlight. Humidity radiated off the sidewalk. Sweat coated her cheeks in an instant. How fitting. Wasn't she stepping into the fire?

Katherine spotted Ryan Park a short distance away, writing on his clipboard. She took a deep breath and marched over.

"Excuse me, Mr. Park." She stood in front of him, her arms akimbo. "I came to warn you I just accepted the position of Lanette Johnson's campaign manager."

"I beg your pardon?" His sleek, black eyebrows dipped.

"I've heard politics is a dirty business, but I hope we can keep this a clean fight. I'm willing if you are." She held out a hand. "What do you say? May the best man or woman win?"

The morning breeze hit her as she waited for his response. Was it her imagination, or did she see a flash of pity cross his face? He must consider her an uneducated rube, but he'd find out soon enough what she could do with a little brainpower and a lot of guts.

He laughed and took her fingers in his. "Challenge accepted."

Katherine steeled herself against the electric sensation where his skin touched hers. He was her opponent, and everyone knew you didn't fraternize with the enemy. She shook his hand once. Hard. And let go.

Time to join forces with Lanette. Her brain spun as she turned away from the opposition. Slogans. Marketing. Campaign Headquarters. So much to do. And only the good Lord knew what awaited them.

Chapter Three

K atherine drove her ancient sedan into a space outside the
abandoned real estate office and killed the engine. The
one-story building sat on a popular stretch of Main Street. She
grabbed the handle and banged her shoulder into the rickety
door to pop it open.

"Ow!" She rubbed the aching bone.

A shiny, oversized SUV pulled beside her as Katherine exited
the car. Her new employer checked her coral lipstick in the
vanity mirror before joining her in the parking lot. Lanette gave
her the once-over, tugged the lopsided hem of Katherine's T-shirt
in place, and spread her arms to the building in front of them.

"Ta-da! Doesn't it scream campaign headquarters?"

A patriotic mural stretched to the left of the storefront
window. It covered a large part of the brick wall. Katherine
cringed at the picture of Lady Liberty with hot pink hair, dressed
in a star-spangled dress and holding a glass jar full of pastel
hearts with messages such as "You're sweet" and "Be mine."

"The jar was my idea." Lanette gave a proud nod. "I wanted
to plug our annual Candy Hearts Festival with an old-fashioned
Americana theme. The tourists love taking pictures here. How
do you like it?"

Katherine's lips turned down. "I—"

"It's ideal." Lanette clapped her hands together. "The perfect place for our headquarters. I used to think the tax write-off wasn't worth the hassle, but I'm glad Harry and I bought it." She inserted a key in the door. It opened with a loud creak. "There's gobs of space for meetings and campaign whatevers."

Katherine swallowed her objections. She wouldn't have to stare at the gaudy mural when she was in the office, and the price was perfect. Free. One less expense to drain the campaign treasury they didn't possess.

She followed Lanette inside to a large, almost-empty room. A few pieces of battered furniture sat in odd spots, patches of cement floor peeked through holes in the cracked linoleum, and spiderwebs adorned the tarnished brass candelabra hanging from the ceiling.

"I know it's not in the best shape, but there's a bathroom in the back." Lanette clicked her tongue and pointed at a beat-up desk by the window. "Oh, that has to go. I've got a better one in my garage. I refurbished it myself with an electric sander. Gave it a classy, distressed style and stenciled rosebuds on the front."

Rosebuds? Katherine restrained her shudder. She'd never been the girly type. A three-legged chair leaned against the wall, and she slipped her gray purse strap over the top. "Don't bother. I've worked with worse."

"Suit yourself." Lanette took out her phone. "I'll get Harry to bring the rest of the furniture. We need somewhere decent to sit when we have our strategy sessions."

"You're going to make him bring the furniture for his rival's office?"

"Who else?" She tapped out a text on the screen. "He was my husband before he was the mayor."

She couldn't argue with Lanette's marital expertise. Katherine pulled a rubber band from her pocket and tugged her hair into a loose ponytail. Where to start? She spotted a closet, opened the door, and found a broom.

"I'll straighten the place while we wait."

Katherine worked for an hour, sweeping, dusting the desk, and swiping the cobwebs off the light fixtures. A major deep clean was required, but at least it no longer resembled a haunted house at the carnival. She pushed another piece of broken tile to the dust pile she'd gathered in the center of the room. A heavy sigh escaped her lips. Was she a campaign manager or a janitor? Her stomach growled, and she cast a glance at her employer.

Lanette stood at the wide window facing Main Street. "Where is that man? Probably talking up a storm with the boys in the barbershop." She slapped the sill. "No point waiting around. Let's go buy lunch and a few cleaning supplies."

The broom clattered to the ground as Katherine grabbed her purse. "You're the boss."

RYAN SCOOPED the last bit of broken tile into the dustpan and dumped it in the trashcan. He propped the broom in a corner and surveyed the room. Not the fanciest office he'd ever worked in, but it had plenty of space to coordinate volunteers. And it was smack dab in the middle of Main Street with a large glass window to generate interest from the passers-by. Always the most important thing.

He jogged out to his car. The stars-and-stripes painting on the wall caught his eye and made him chuckle. It perfectly summed up his expectations for this campaign. A political farce with sentimental speeches and a splash of Americana. He withdrew a box from the front seat, carried it inside, and deposited it on the desk.

An SUV pulled into the space out front. He watched as Lanette Johnson climbed from behind the wheel and Katherine scooted from the passenger's side with two overflowing paper bags in her arms. The women walked to the building's entrance. Were they checking out the competition?

"Ladies," Ryan met them at the door, "what an unexpected pleasure." He noted the way the afternoon sun highlighted the red tints in Katherine's brown hair and realized his words weren't mere flattery. Why was he so glad to see the rival campaign manager?

Perhaps glad wasn't the right word. Energized?

She peeked over the bags with a furrowed brow. "What are you doing here?"

He gestured at the space behind him. "Setting up my office."

Lanette squawked. "*Your* office?"

"Yes." His smile faded a bit. "Mayor Johnson told me to use this for his headquarters."

"That man!" Lanette stomped a pink, high-heeled cowboy boot. "He's getting sneaky in his old age. I bet he waited until we were gone before he called you."

Katherine bent and set the bags on the floor. She rose and drew herself to her full height. "I'm sorry to disappoint you, Mr. Park, but we've already claimed this space for Lanette's campaign."

His outward demeanor stayed calm, but inside he was groaning. Was this going to be his life for the next two months? Sparring round after round with this spitfire until the election? When he returned to New York, he should ask for a raise.

Ryan quirked an eyebrow. "The mayor said the property was in his name."

"Oh, it's in his name, all right." Lanette unzipped her purse and took out her pink, bedazzled phone. "But he neglected to mention mine is right next to his." She dialed the cell and stormed to the exit. "Catch you later, Katie. I've got a husband to strangle."

The door slammed so hard it rattled the candelabra over their heads.

Katherine motioned to the ceiling. "Cobwebs decorated those lights until I wiped them off."

He gazed at the brass fixture. "Thanks for saving me time. I never did enjoy cleaning."

The muscle in her jaw popped as she waved at the floor. "This was covered with grime and broken tiles. Did you think a sweeping fairy came in and made the dust pile?"

"Again," Ryan grinned, "thanks."

He knew he was being shameless, but it was important to seize the high ground in a battle. If he wanted to blow a hole in the opposition's campaign, he needed to knock Lanette's manager off-kilter.

Ryan pulled his wallet from his pocket and opened it. "I'd be willing to reimburse you for your time. You did a nice job tidying up the place."

"Why you—" Katherine's cheeks turned a deep shade of red as her hands gripped into fists at her sides. "I'm not your maid, you addlepated sexist. And if you don't get out of my headquarters in one minute, I may do something I'll have to confess to the preacher on Sunday. Not that I'll be sorry for it." She took one step toward him.

He forced himself to remain still. She wouldn't resort to violence, would she? He'd been in big city campaigns where he had to watch his back, but with this woman, he'd have to watch his front, side, and everything else.

"Remember the old adage." Ryan tucked his wallet away. "Possession is nine-tenths of the law." He pointed at the campaign poster he'd attached to the cracked plaster wall.

A giant picture of Mayor Johnson beamed over the office like a beatific angel. The slogan *Harry has heart* filled the bottom in giant red letters. Red was a power color.

Katherine eyed the poster with a curled lip. She headed for the wall, but a ringing from her purse stopped her. Ryan's phone buzzed at the exact same time. They both found their cells and answered.

"Hello?" Katherine pulled the phone away as Lanette's irritated bellow echoed from the speaker.

"Hi, Mayor." Ryan marked every move she made. He wouldn't put it past her to try and rip the poster off the wall.

They stared each other down as they listened to the people on their phones.

"Are you crazy?" Katherine's volume rose to match her employer's.

Ryan plugged a finger in the ear closest to her and turned away. "Mayor Johnson, you might want to reconsider."

After several minutes of frustrated mumbling from him and loud protests from Katherine, they hung up.

She faced him with a frown. "You heard?"

He gave a short nod. "Seems like we're sharing."

Katherine snorted in disgust.

Ryan walked to the antiquated desk by the window. Rummaging through the box, he drew out a pad of yellow sticky notes and wrote. He peeled off the paper and stuck it to the aged blotter on top. She eyed it with suspicion, stomped over, and read the words.

Property of Ryan Park.

Katherine swiped the note and held it in front of his nose. "What's this?"

"A friendly reminder." He leaned away. "I find working relationships are easier to maintain with clearly defined boundaries."

He scribbled on another piece of paper and placed it on the rolling chair. "Mayor Johnson told me to use anything I found in the office."

She propped her hands on her hips. "And where am I supposed to sit?"

His gaze darted around the room. It landed on a folded-up card table and a three-legged chair shoved in a far corner. He pointed. "Help yourself."

Katherine's mouth popped open and snapped shut again. She sucked air through her gritted teeth and closed her eyes. He'd bet his life she was counting to ten. His breath stuttered from his nose, but he tried to hold it in. Laughter would make the situation worse.

She was cute when she was mad.

Her lids raised, and she spoke slowly. "This property is as much Lanette's as it is her husband's. If we're both using it, we'll have to share the resources."

Ryan wrote as he answered. "That's going to be awkward. Mayor Johnson and I have this place booked for the next month. Strategy meetings. Canvassing planning. Volunteer coordination. I'm afraid there aren't enough supplies for both of us." He slipped the note from the stack and stuck it on the whiteboard.

Clang!

Katherine kicked the metal trash can by the desk. "I'm sure you've noticed, Mister Park, I'm a little short in the patience department. Thanks to you, I've already broken my resolution about holding my tongue, so I might as well let it all out."

He spotted a bevy of golden flecks in her green eyes. Were they always there? Or did they only ignite when she was angry?

She stepped right under his nose as if to give him a better look. "You're soft in the head if you think I'll let you steal this election like you stole my desk."

"*Your* desk?"

"You may boast the political experience and the big-city contacts, but I've got something you can't buy in a million years."

He raised an eyebrow in response and waited.

"I've got a lifetime in Sweetheart to draw from. Until you've breathed the same air as these people for thirty years, you can't begin to understand the way they feel."

She was right.

Although he'd never admit it. Insider knowledge was priceless, but he could handle it. Ryan raised the pen and tapped her nose, wanting to see the sparks in her eyes one more time. They exploded as he'd hoped.

"Thanks for the warning." He scribbled another note. "I'll keep my guard up."

He tore off the paper and pasted it to the lip of the metal trash can.

Property of Ryan Park. Please refrain from kicking.

"Now, if you'll excuse me. I need to place an order for handbills." He walked to the exit as she followed closer than a tailgater on the New Jersey Turnpike. Maybe the tenacious Katherine would take the hint if he opened the door.

She didn't.

He flexed his hand on the knob. "Can we continue this later? Sweetheart needs to hear about the progressive plans Mayor Johnson has for his town."

"I'm not finished."

Ryan took out his wallet and withdrew a business card. "Please give me a call later."

He slipped it in her fingers, edged outside, and shut the door with a gentle click behind him. Despite his calm exterior, Ryan's heart jerked like a jackhammer. Working in the political field, he was used to confrontation. Yet something about the woman had upset his even keel. But what?

Maintaining a safe distance was difficult when they shared a workspace. Should he spin the close quarters to his advantage? It was obvious from their first encounter at the community center the woman was attracted to him. If she hadn't caught him spewing sexist nonsense to the men at the meeting, Katherine might still be admiring him with all the fervor of an infatuated teenager. If he worked hard to mend their social fences, he could make her fall again. And a woman with a crush was a distracted woman—thinking about romance, not campaigns.

Ryan looked at the closed glass door. Katherine stood on the other side, glaring at him. He turned his smile on full voltage and leveled it at her. Her eyebrows raised in confusion. He held his thumb and pinky to his ear in the gesture people who were born before cell phones used.

Call me, he mouthed.

Bewilderment spread across her face. He waved with both hands and turned to hide his laughter. Whether this flirtation won her over or merely confused her didn't matter. A winning political strategy used every trick in the book.

Chapter Four

A translucent mist floated above the grass in front of the rundown bungalow on Quincy Street. The low-hanging fog drifted in an eerie, serpentine pattern as a breeze caught the rusty windchimes hanging from the porch. Their high-pitched tinkle echoed in the early morning darkness.

Katherine shivered and rubbed her sweatshirt-clad arms. "Why did you drag me here?"

No answer.

"Don't pretend you're innocent. I need more sleep after moving a roomful of furniture for Lanette. I'd still be in bed if it weren't for you."

A cheerful bark. Followed by two furry bodies running around her legs.

"Stop tangling your leashes!"

Katherine tried to maneuver out of the nylon spiderweb before she tripped. The foster dogs she'd agreed to keep for a month ignored her instructions. The tiny, black Yorkies spun and yipped and chased each other's tails without any regard for the inconvenient hour.

"If you don't behave, I'll take you back to the shelter."

Empty threats, and they knew it. The puppies bounced on top of each other and rolled in the dew-covered grass.

Katherine rubbed her eyes. "Please finish your business and let me sleep a few more minutes before I meet Lanette."

And Ryan Park. He'd be at the office too.

The thought made her want to dive in bed and hide under the covers. It wasn't because she was scared of him. No, not scared. Aware. He unnerved her in a new and intoxicating way. She was used to getting mad and blowing up at people, but Ryan touched a different chord. Mixed with the anger was an electric spark she wanted to deny.

And couldn't.

She'd never been adept at controlling her emotions. Would it be the same with attraction? They'd work in close quarters for hours at a time. Day after day. What if she blurted out something embarrassing?

"Get a grip, Katherine. No fraternizing with the enemy."

The Yorkies sniffed along the ramshackle fence. She eyed the old Wilkerson place on the other side. No one had lived there since the elderly owner passed away six years ago. It used to be a cute little cottage, but neglect had stripped the paint from the boards and torn the shingles from the roof. She'd like to buy the house and pour some tender loving care into it.

If she could only find a job that matched her personality and paid well. She doubted her current occupation fit the bill. Lanette would regret hiring her. Politics weren't made for a person with Katherine's handicap—Big Mouth Disease. Wasn't everyone in the political field supposed to be smarmy and self-controlled?

Like Ryan Park.

No time for daydreams. She'd better get to work if she wanted to beat her experienced rival.

Katherine cast one last look at the cottage.

"Someday," she whispered to the darling little place. "Wait for me."

A SHRILL BARK woke Ryan from his exhausted sleep. Was there a dog in his apartment? Impossible. He lifted his head off the pillow and squinted in the darkness at the unfamiliar room. He'd spent his first night in town at the Sweetheart Inn until his employer got permanent lodgings ready. Mayor Johnson had dropped him off at two in the morning, and he'd barely glanced at the new place before finding the bedroom and lapsing into a coma. Ryan dragged himself off the mattress and stumbled into the small living room of the duplex.

Yipping sounded from the front porch. Was it a stray? He padded barefoot to the door and yanked it open.

A woman stood with her back to him in mismatched sweats with the hood over her head. Two Yorkies ran around her feet, tangling their leash lines.

Ryan yawned. "Can I help you?"

The hood dropped as she turned, revealing a thick chestnut ponytail.

"Mr. Park?" Katherine Bruno gaped. She took him in from head to toe.

He ran a self-conscious hand through his mangled, spiky bed hair. His sleep-fogged brain tried to process the situation. Why was she standing on his porch before dawn? Was this a business call? In sweatpants?

"Good morning." His voice sounded rough to his own ears. "What are you doing here?"

"I live here."

"You what?" Ryan stepped onto the porch. The scorching concrete floor sent tiny heatwaves through his toes. Didn't it ever cool down in this town?

Katherine motioned to the door beside his, leading to the other half of the duplex. She was his neighbor? He wanted to smack his forehead.

She scooped the tiny dogs up, one in each arm. "I live next

door. Mayor Johnson and Lanette own this place, so I can guess what happened. Were room and board included in your job description?"

"Yes—that is—yes."

She nodded.

He nodded back, shifting his weight from one hot foot to the other.

A suffocating blanket of awkward silence dropped around them. The rattle of a passing train sounded from far away. Ryan grasped the doorknob and waited.

"I see." She clutched the squirming puppies to her chest, and one of them yipped. "This is Bella and Romeo. I'm fostering them for the local shelter. They're a handful, but—" Her sentence trailed off in a nervous dribble.

"Cute. The dogs." He waved at the Yorkies. The one with the pink bow in its fur whined and stretched his way. He reached out and gave the animal's head a quick rub.

Katherine's green eyes lit with a sudden gleam. "You'll be in town until the election. Why don't you foster a puppy?"

"You want to shove your dog off on me?" Ryan retreated into his apartment.

"Not Bella and Romeo." She advanced. "There are others at the shelter who need a home. The commitment is only for a month, and it will keep you from getting lonely."

"I'm not at all lonely. Besides, I'm too busy with the mayor's campaign."

"I'm keeping two dogs at my apartment, and I still manage to get everything done."

"Congratulations. You're an admirable foster parent." He started to close the door. "I hope you three will be very happy together."

"Wait!"

He paused and peered at her through the crack.

Katherine raised her chin. "The last tenant was way too fond of heavy metal. I hope you'll keep the noise down."

The barking resumed as she stomped off and entered her apartment. Ryan stuck his head out and stared at her closing door. *He* should keep the noise down?

First, he had to work with this crazy woman. Now he had to live beside her. What kind of twisted providence kept throwing this touchy shrew into his path?

Ryan spent the next hour tossing and turning. How could he sleep knowing who lived in the other half of the duplex? He kicked the sheet off, climbed out of bed, and dressed. Time to drive to the new office and get some work done. If Katherine arrived first, she might ignore his sticky note dibs and claim the desk for herself.

Not one soul appeared on his drive through town at five in the morning. Ryan parked in front of the darkened office and soaked in the stillness. So different from New York. Sweetheart rested in gentle repose, content to sleep until the sun came up. He stuck the key Mayor Johnson gave him in the front door, entered the darkened room, and felt along the wall for a light switch.

His shoe connected with something. It clunked like pottery, and he stumbled. A sharp metal object poked him in the side. He didn't remember any furniture near the doorway. Sliding his hand up, he found the switch and squinted as light from the candelabra flooded the room. An intricate brass coat rack was the culprit. A cacophony of dainty hats covered the hooks. He sniffed as the syrupy scent of potpourri drifted past his nose.

Ryan turned slowly and blanched. A chintz sofa of navy and pink stripes with gardenia accents sat in the middle of the room. Lacy throw pillows rested in a neat row across the cushions. A coffee table perched in the middle flanked by brocade-covered chairs, and an elegant tea service rested on top.

It was so delicate. So unprofessional. So pink.

He shuddered. What had she done with his things? Ryan spotted his beat-up desk jammed in the corner with the yellow sticky note still stuck to it. A dainty, beige escritoire with rosebuds painted on the legs sat in his former spot near the window.

Ryan strode through the room and stopped at the feminine desk. A sticky note sat on top. A pink sticky note. It read:

Property of Katherine Bruno.

Move it, and you'll wish you hadn't.

Ryan pushed his sleeves up and bent. Grabbing the lightweight furniture, he lifted it an inch off the floor but hesitated. Was it worth it? The warning the old man at the community center gave him on the first night rang in his ears.

Best beware her sting!

He returned the desk and straightened. What did it matter where he worked? Winning a campaign against a small-town pretender who didn't know a swing vote from a porch swing was child's play.

Ryan turned, and a movement outside caught his attention. Someone across the street backed a vehicle into the alley opposite his office—headlights off. Whoever it was moved fast enough, he couldn't tell if it was a man or a woman.

The radar developed from a lifetime in the big city sounded an alert. He moved closer to the window. They rolled up the sidewalks in this town at nine o'clock and didn't open until the sun came out. Who was this person skulking in the shadows?

Ryan watched for several minutes, but no one appeared. He shook his head. This was Sweetheart, not New York. No need to imagine problems where they didn't exist. Enough real challenges filled his plate. And any minute, the biggest one would walk through the door with her ponytail swinging.

Chapter Five

"Smell that?" Katherine took a deep breath of humid air as she stretched her arms to the clouds. "It's the scent of victory."

Rosy orange streaks painted the lowest edges of the horizon, and the soft outline of a new moon still hung high in the sky. Birds perched on the decorative black lampposts. Their cheerful morning ditties echoed up and down Main Street.

Elise yawned wide enough to expose the gold filling in her last molar. "Couldn't we smell it a little later? There's hardly anyone out at this hour. Who are we supposed to—what did you call it—canvas?"

"If we get an early start, we'll be sure to catch everyone doing their weekend shopping." Katherine tucked the hem of her white Oxford shirt in the waistband of her black knee-length skirt. She had no idea how a campaign manager dressed, but this outfit seemed professional. "Lanette can talk to people and shake a few hands."

"Not if she's not here." Elise wrapped her lightweight, multicolored sweater around her wide body. "I suppose she expects us to do all the work again, and she'll mosey on in whenever—"

A familiar white SUV drove beside them and parked at the curb. Lanette honked her horn and waved from the driver's seat. Elise pressed her lips together in a guilty pucker.

"Don't worry." Katherine patted her arm. "There's no way she heard you."

Their stylish candidate climbed from the car and buttoned the jacket of her hot pink power suit. She slipped on a pair of matching sunglasses and smoothed the sides of her blonde bob as she leaned against the open door.

Elise scrambled to her side. "Oh, honey, you look so pretty."

"Sorry, ladies. The hairdresser came to my house, but it took a little longer than expected. Are you ready to make some political waves?"

"Yes, ma'am." Katherine pointed at the stores and restaurants along the thoroughfare. "This is the busiest spot in Sweetheart on Saturdays. We can spend the morning walking around, talking to voters."

"Good plan." Lanette gestured to her white patent leather pumps. "Except for the walking part. I've got a bunion on my right foot that won't stand for it. How about we find someplace to settle and let the voters come to us?"

Katherine shrugged a shoulder. "I guess we can make it work. You sit at a table outside Rosa's Taqueria, and I'll direct people your way."

"Perfect." She reached into her car and withdrew a color-coordinated pink seat cushion. "Let's stake our claim before Harry gets here. Last night, I overheard him on the phone with his manager. They'll be showing up later. Katie, there's a box of flyers I had Wilbur print for me in the trunk. Be a dear and grab them. They're nothing fancy, just a good picture of me and the words *Vote for Lanette*."

She slammed the car door and clipped across the street. Elise scurried after her, and Katherine rolled her eyes.

"First order of business—create a decent slogan." Katherine

yanked open the door. She hefted the box onto one hip. "I've got to be the manager, the ad person, and the muscle."

Stalking after her candidate, she reached the restaurant as Lanette dragged a wrought iron table closer to the curb and deposited her cushion on a chair.

Katherine plopped the box on the sidewalk and surveyed the quiet street. Where would a hotshot political consultant set up? Was this the best location?

Too late. Lanette was already sinking into her seat for the duration.

Katherine pulled her phone from her pocket. "I'll text Rosa and make sure it's okay with her."

Lanette sniffed at the iron table. "Let's spruce it up a little. A tablecloth and flowers. I want my campaign first class."

Katherine finished the text, slipped a chocolate mint from her pocket, and unwrapped the silver paper. Why had she skipped breakfast? This was going to be a long day.

Her boss motioned at the restaurant and squinted. "What are those tacky papers on the window? Elise, be a dear and take care of the mess."

"Yes, Lanette." Elise walked to the offensive signs. She reached to grab one and gasped. "Oh, my!"

Katherine shoved the candy in her mouth. "Problem?"

She spun around and stretched her arms wide. "Don't come over here."

"What is it?" Lanette ignored the advice, rose, and started in her friend's direction.

"Trust me. You don't want to see this." Elise danced right and left as if her moving body might distract the woman.

Lanette marched over and pushed her aside. "If it involves the campaign, I have to—"

She froze. A mortified squeak escaped her lips.

Katherine put her phone away and joined them. Her teeth clenched at the sight. Grainy black-and-white photocopies stuck to the large window of the taqueria. She heard a laugh down the street and saw two men in cowboy hats pointing at the mercantile. Papers fluttered in the breeze from the windows of every business on Main Street, and a common theme connected them all—Lanette Johnson at her worst.

Hunched over a plate of barbecue with her cheeks bulging. Yelling into a bullhorn at an army of festival workers. Sitting in a salon chair with her chin strap in place.

Lanette stumbled along the sidewalk, absorbing the gallery of humiliation. Elise followed behind with her arms outstretched like she expected her friend to faint dead away. Katherine brought up the rear. Her gaze swung from one side of the street to the other. What a spiteful, mean-spirited trick to pull. Ryan Park would never stoop this low.

Would he?

The trio stopped at the end of Main Street where a statue of the town's founder, Amos P. Colter, stood in the middle of the square. A vinyl banner covered the six-foot marble pedestal at the bottom. The final life-sized picture showed Lanette without a stitch of makeup, wearing a frayed flannel bathrobe, hair sticking out six ways to Sunday, with her sagging jaws guzzling a giant mug of coffee.

"Have mercy," Elise whimpered.

Katherine cringed and supported Lanette's elbow. The woman's lower jaw jutted out, and her eyes were mere slits as she glared at the banner.

Her raspy voice was whisper soft with a thread of steel. "Girls, this is gonna get ugly."

"MISTER PARK!"

Ryan sighed and closed his laptop. He'd hoped to offer a few friendly overtures to his competitor and buy her a cup of coffee, but she'd walked through the door yelling at full volume. So much for civility.

He spun his desk chair and stood. "Good morning, Katherine."

She pitched her gray purse a foot away, where it bounced off the chintz-covered couch and rolled to the floor. "You've been hard at work."

"Yes." He smiled. "I'm at my most productive in the first half of the day."

"I saw the evidence up and down Main Street." She stomped over and shoved a wrinkled paper in his face.

He tried to focus on the picture an inch from his nose. It wasn't a good one—a cheap photocopy of Lanette Johnson with her mouth full.

Ryan smirked. "I shouldn't give advice to the opposition, but if you're considering this for a campaign poster, I wouldn't recommend it."

Katherine crumpled it in her fist and chucked it at his head. He dodged and put a safer distance between them. Did this woman have any other setting besides outraged? His brain spun through the possible catalysts for this new tantrum. Could it be because he'd refused to foster a dog? Or was she still upset about sharing the office?

Walking to the other side of the couch, he studied her wide, furious eyes. No. This was a new level of outrage—even for her.

"I think I'm missing something."

She followed. "A conscience? I can't believe Mayor Johnson authorized such sneaky, despicable tactics."

He edged around the couch corner. "Hold on." His foot caught on the Persian rug and he stumbled.

Katherine stalked him through the office, cornering him between his desk and the wall. Cold concrete pressed against his spine. She planted her hand beside his head. The urge to laugh hit him. He felt like the bullied outcast in a teenage melodrama.

"Katherine, use your words. What sneaky, despicable thing are you referring to?"

"The scandalous pictures of Lanette posted on every store

window in Sweetheart. Is this a trick they taught you in your big city campaigns?"

He straightened. "I had nothing to do with any pictures."

How dare she storm in here with zero proof and accuse him of underhanded tactics? Was that the kind of person she saw him as?

He tried to scoot to the side. "I resent the implication and suggest you look elsewhere for the culprit."

"I'm not finished." Katherine blocked his way with her other hand. "If you didn't put those pictures up, who did? Someone on your team?"

"I don't have a team." His voice rose, and he fought for control. He would not allow this small-town hothead to drag him into the emotional muck. "But I will soon, and I can assure you they will operate in an ethical manner. Whoever heckled your candidate did not do so under my direction."

She remained in front of him, feet spread apart. Taking his measure.

Ryan drew a calming breath and inhaled the scent of chocolate mint. He studied her expression and noted a tiny dark smudge at the corner of her lip. He raised his index finger but paused.

Would she slap him? His inner machismo goaded him on. Was he afraid of a girl? He swiped at the remnant.

Katherine tucked in her chin and lowered her hands. "What are you doing?"

He wagged the brown smudge on his fingertip. "Chocolate for breakfast?"

Before she could answer, he grasped her shoulders and swung her around to his previous position against the wall. Placing one hand on the exact spot she'd used, he leaned down to search for those familiar golden sparks in her green eyes.

There they were.

Time for a little payback.

~

KATHERINE'S BELLY VIBRATED.

Was she breathing? Her brain was skittering around too much to check. The intimate proximity of Ryan Park short-circuited everything but her heart, which was alive and well. Thump-thumping away in her chest.

Katherine barely moved her lips to speak. "I find this very uncomfortable."

"My sentiments exactly." His tall frame hovered over her. He placed his other hand on the opposite side of her head. "May I remind you, Ms. Bruno, I was in this same predicament a few seconds ago while you railed at me?"

She pressed back, but the unforgiving wall left no room for retreat. Perhaps she had gone a bit too far.

He thumbed a finger at the door. "If anyone were to walk in, they might misunderstand this unseemly pose. Don't you think?"

She gave short nods, still trying not to bump into the gorgeous face so close to hers. The warm air from his nostrils skittered across her cheek.

"I'm glad you agree." He lowered his arms, but his face remained centimeters from her own.

A flurry of scenes from her favorite romantic movies sped through her mind. Would this situation end the same way? With a kiss? Anticipation lodged in her throat.

"From now on," his gaze dropped to her lips for the briefest second and snapped up to her eyes, "let's keep things professional."

He moved away and walked to the window. The cold air rushed to fill the space where he'd stood. Katherine sagged. Whether with relief or disappointment, she wasn't sure.

Ryan clasped his hands behind him. "You say the pictures were posted on the storefronts?"

"Pictures?" What was he talking about? Oh, right. Lanette! "Yes, they're taped along Main Street."

"I arrived at the office at five a.m. It must have happened earlier."

Katherine tugged the cotton lapels of her shirt collar together. "Makes sense."

She joined him at the window, a foot of space between them. It was still early, and very few people strolled along the sidewalk.

Ryan took an almost imperceptible step away from her and leaned closer to the glass. "Are there any security cameras?"

"In Sweetheart? What for?"

He pointed at the alley. "I noticed someone skulking in the shadows over there when I arrived."

"Who?"

"Couldn't even tell if it was a man or a woman."

Katherine huffed in frustration and thunked a fist against the glass. She didn't want this stupid job in the first place, and now she had to play detective.

If Ryan hadn't orchestrated the mortifying photo gallery, who was behind it? And what possible motive could that person have for making Lanette Johnson the town laughingstock?

Chapter Six

K atherine collapsed on a wooden stool, leaned her arms on the counter, and buried her face in her hands.

"I saw the pictures." Deanna Day flitted over in her vintage cardigan and pencil skirt like the ghost of a 1950s bobbysoxer. "Yikes!"

The soda fountain museum was one of the quirkier spots in Sweetheart. Not to be outdone by its equally unique proprietress. Katherine's best friend lived every day as if she'd tap-danced out of a black-and-white movie. Deanna nodded her head in sympathy, but the golden victory rolls on top didn't move. How much hair spray did she use anyway?

"Everyone saw the pictures." Katherine moaned. "Hundreds of them! I ran around collecting as many as I could, but the word was already out. People drove into town to see them."

"Here." Deanna pulled a bottle of root beer from the fridge under the counter, grabbed an opener, and popped off the metal cap. "I'll spot you a drink on the house."

Katherine wrapped her fingers around the chilly, brown glass. "Why did I take this job?"

"Why *did* you?"

"I must have lost my mind." She took a long draught of root

beer and slammed the bottle down. An arc of fizzy soda splashed on the counter. "Ryan Park got me worked up about the new town hall, and I said yes to Lanette before I knew what I was doing."

"Ryan who?" Deanna tugged a red-and-white checkered cloth off the hook beside the cash register and dabbed at the spill.

"Some guy from New York City the mayor hired to run his campaign."

"Oh, I saw him at the meeting on Thursday." She sighed. "What a dreamboat."

"More like a nightmare. I've lost track of how many run-ins we've had already. He's arrogant but smart. It won't be easy to beat him."

"What's this?" Her friend clasped her fingers under her chin and leaned forward with a glint in her eye. "A man who doesn't cower at the sight of you? Sounds promising. Do you feel any sparks when he's around?"

"Sparks? I feel a whole forest fire—of rage. Do you know he backed me up—" Katherine stopped. If she told Deanna the details, she'd have to admit she'd started the whole thing. "Never mind. I need to show this guy we aren't a bunch of small-town hicks who will dance to whatever tune he plays. And you're going to help."

"Me?" The young woman's cherry red lips scrunched in a babydoll pout. "I hate politics. Please don't ask me to get involved." She stuck her hands in the pockets of her skirt and hunched her shoulders. "Besides, it's been busier at the museum of late. More tourists this year."

Katherine cast a glance around the room. Old phonographs, metal advertisement signs, and antique memorabilia filled the former pharmacy. Not a person in sight. A burnished wooden counter stretched down the side, and a myriad of drawers where the pills used to be kept filled the wall. Did any of them hold an aspirin?

She eyed her friend. "Looks empty to me."

Deanna sidled away. "A customer might walk in at any minute." The bell above the door jingled, and her face brightened. "There's someone now!"

She hurried to the front—Katherine close on her heels. Ryan stood by the entrance, taking in the cluttered room.

"Welcome!" Deanna latched on to his forearm as if she feared he'd disappear. "You're the visitor from New York, correct? I'd be happy to give you a museum tour for as long as you please."

"You're too kind," he smiled, "but I hoped to speak with you about Mayor Johnson's campaign."

She yanked away like he was contagious. "More politics."

He noted Katherine standing behind her. "Ah, I'm not the first here. I can visit another time if it's more convenient."

"It will never be convenient." Deanna shook her head so hard her blonde victory rolls bounced. "Telling me to choose between Uncle Harry and Aunt Lanette is the equivalent of asking a child if they love their father or mother more."

"Uncle Harry?" Ryan's expression went blank.

Katherine stepped up. "They're not real kin, but Deanna's mom and Lanette grew up together."

Deanna moved behind the counter. "They're as close as any real family I've got." She slapped the wooden bar. "And I refuse to hurt either of them."

Ryan gave her a thumbs up. "Your loyalty is admirable. But surely it wouldn't hurt your Uncle Harry's feelings if you hung his campaign poster in your window."

"True." She tilted her head as if considering it.

Katherine shouldered in front of Ryan. "What about your Aunt Lanette? How would it make her feel?"

Deanna flinched. "Also true."

Katherine walked around the counter and locked arms with her. "Hanging Lanette's poster will not only make *her* happy but also one of your oldest dearest friends."

"Who?"

"I mean me, you—" Katherine bit her tongue before she lambasted her oldest dearest friend.

Ryan leaned over the counter. "Think of Uncle Harry. He needs your support."

Deanna looked between them and tried to shake Katherine off. "You win."

"Who wins?" Katherine squeezed tighter.

"Both of you." Deanna freed herself and opened her arms in a welcoming gesture. "I'll put Uncle Harry *and* Aunt Lanette's posters in the window. The good people of Sweetheart can decide between them."

Ryan recovered faster than Katherine.

"I appreciate your consideration, and I'm sure Uncle Harry will too. I'll stop by tomorrow with the poster." He nodded at Katherine. "Ms. Bruno, a pleasure as always."

Where was he headed? Ryan Park possessed years of experience she couldn't begin to match. Her own inadequacy taunted her. She was barely treading water. Were there tricks of the trade she could learn from him?

Katherine took another swig from her root beer and shoved the bottle at her friend. "Thanks, Dee. I'll bring Lanette's poster once we have it printed. We'll be leaving now."

"Whoa." Ryan raised a hand. "I wasn't inviting you to join me."

"I know. But I'm coming anyway."

"Why?"

"I have no experience as a campaign manager." She walked to his side. "So, I'll tail you until I figure it out."

He motioned at Deanna with a beseeching frown.

"Sorry, mister." She grabbed the half-empty bottle and shooed him away. "I've known Katherine thirty years, and I still can't make her do anything. It's easier to give in and save yourself time."

"But," he skirted around a display case of vinyl records, "I'm the opposition."

"You said it yourself." Katherine tracked his every move, standing opposite him on the other side. "You're the best."

Ryan stopped with a self-assured quirk of his lips. He planted his hands on the glass top and bent across it. "Can you keep up with me?"

She mirrored his stance until they were nose-to-nose. "Try me."

"*Mm-mmm.*" Deanna's cheeky hum floated through the room. "Looks like today's going to be a hot one."

RYAN STOOD on the sidewalk outside the museum and scanned his surroundings. How was he supposed to recruit volunteers with Katherine shadowing him? He turned his attention to the bright blue sky overhead. It stretched for miles in every direction without a single skyscraper to block the sunlight.

"What are we doing?" Katherine tapped her sneakered foot on the pavement. "Aren't you supposed to be canvassing or whatever they call it?"

"I will. But first, I want to get a read on the town. Check the water level in the pool before I dive in."

She made a face. "Wish I'd done more checking in my life. I would have collected fewer bumps on my head."

He chuckled and waved for her to go first. She took off at a fast clip, walking near the curb.

Ryan caught up, placed a gentle hand on her elbow, and nudged her over. "My mother taught me the gentleman walks closest to the street so he can be the first to get run over."

Her lips twitched. "Manners are murder."

They walked along in silence, passing the main square where a pigeon landed on the head of the founder's statue. Loudspeakers on the telephone poles played a cheerful mix of Fifties pop music, Motown, and classic rock-and-roll.

Were all small towns this picturesque, or was it only

Sweetheart? Black iron lampposts with matching benches lined the street, and stone flowerpots with a giant Texas star on the side overflowed with colorful peonies. A proprietor sang at full volume as he arranged jars of homemade jalapeño jelly on a table in front of his store.

Katherine headed toward him. "Hello, Mr. Torres."

"Howdy, Katie."

"Are you planning to vote for Lanette in the election?"

"Look at the time." New wrinkles appeared on his forehead. "I should take my break." He pulled out a painted sign which read, *Leave your money in the basket if you buy something.*

Ryan eyed the trusting message. Where he came from, the money and the jelly would both be gone before Mr. Torres returned.

Katherine hollered at the man scurrying away. "I'll come by and see you later."

"Yoo-hoo." A sing-songy voice called behind them. "Kaaaa-tie!"

Katherine grimaced. She heaved a long-suffering sigh before spinning around. "Hello, Renae."

Ryan turned. A tall blonde in jeans that looked like she'd need a shoehorn to get them on waved from a salon doorway. Her red stiletto heels *click-clicked* against the sidewalk as she waddled toward them.

"It's been ages since we've hung out, Katie." Though she spoke to Katherine, her heavily mascaraed eyes were pointed at him.

Katherine raised her brows. "Have we ever hung out?"

"Oh, you." She swatted rhinestone-studded fingernails her way. "Stop kidding and introduce me to this attractive stranger."

"Ryan Park, ma'am." He held out a hand. "I'm Mayor Johnson's campaign manager."

Renae took his hand in both of hers. "I've heard about you, but the gossip didn't do you justice, Ryan. Welcome to

Sweetheart. I hope you plan to stay a while. A very long while."
She giggled.

"Until victory is assured." Ryan bestowed a wide grin. "If you fancy being part of a winning campaign, stop by my office. We can always use another talented volunteer."

Katherine made a sound between a choke and a gag.

Renae's gaze cut to her, but her double-rowed smile never wavered. "Thank you, Ryan. I'll be seeing you soon. If you two will excuse me, I have an appointment with my personal stylist. Goodbye, *Katie*."

She twirled away, and Katherine's eyelids shut. Her lips moved for a few seconds, but no sound came out.

Ryan leaned in. "Are you okay?"

"Just telling God all the things I want to say out loud but know I shouldn't." She focused on him. "How about we get to work?"

They strolled along Main Street. A woman in a classic, aqua-blue convertible called a greeting as she drove past. Ryan waited for a group of singing townsfolk carrying fruit baskets to appear and dance around the lampposts at any moment.

He spun in a slow circle. "It's like I time-traveled to 1960. This town reeks of old-fashioned values. Do you ever feel like you're living on a movie set?"

"I might ask you the same. Traipsing through the skyscraper canyons of New York City."

They stopped in front of a two-story building. The white columns stood stark against the weathered red bricks.

"This architecture is beautiful." Ryan studied the historical design. "Do you bank here?"

"It's empty."

He observed the front door. Gold lettering on the glass front announced the hours of the Sweetheart Memorial Bank. "It looks open."

"That's for the tourists' benefit. More than half the businesses on Main Street are pretty facades. The council decided it was more scenic than a bunch of boarded-up stores. They keep the signs turned to *Closed* so no visitors try to enter."

"Clever." He gave an approving thumbs up.

She nodded. "Lanette's idea."

Ryan stepped to the door, shaded his eyes, and peered through the glass. Inside, a small marble-tiled foyer sat with waist-high counters on both sides. At the far end stretched a large staircase which broke into two smaller ones at the landing, leading to the second floor. The thick wooden banisters must have been cut from a whole tree trunk.

"What a waste. It's hard to believe no one wants to buy such a gorgeous building."

Katherine caressed the smooth white column. "It's a little too ornate for everyday use. The city took possession when the bank went under fourteen years ago. Sometimes they'll open it for a special function. Mayor Johnson and Lanette throw an annual Christmas party and decorate the place with more glitter and garland than a home interior magazine. The whole town comes out for the celebration."

"Sounds amazing." He moved away from the door. "It must have been wonderful to grow up in such a tight-knit community. Like one giant family."

"Don't be fooled." She leaned against the column and crossed her arms. "Sweetheart used to be a dump."

"I beg your pardon?"

"I think I was thirteen when things came to a boil. The town wasn't the same in those days. There was litter along the sidewalks. Junky cars parked in people's front yards. Drugs were a big problem."

"Really?" He tried to reconcile the dystopia she painted with the innocent picture postcard in front of him.

"The former mayor was corrupt. He turned a blind eye to anything and everything for a piece of the action. The Johnsons were brave enough to confront him. They led the charge to get him out of office. He didn't just lose an election. They threw him in jail."

"Wow."

"Not taking away from Mayor Johnson's generosity, but the reason he didn't draw a salary in the beginning was because the town couldn't afford to pay him. It took years to restore Sweetheart. The vintage lampposts and fancy iron benches on Main Street? The flower planters? The pride people take in our community? It's thanks to Lanette."

"I concede your point." Ryan squinted and pointed behind her. "Is Mr. Torres coming back?"

"Where?" She straightened from the column and turned.

He ducked down the alley and ran. Slipping behind a large gray dumpster, he crouched.

"Hey!" Katherine's voice hollered after him.

Shoes pounded against the pavement. She was close. If she turned to the right, she'd find him. Ryan held his breath.

"Mr. Park?" she called. The sound of her footsteps grew faint as she ran the other way.

Ryan exhaled. Ditching her in broad daylight didn't work well with his flirtation strategy, but he needed to visit the local editor. An endorsement from the town paper would go a long way for a candidate's campaign, and he didn't want Katherine to realize it. He poked his head around the dumpster.

Empty.

Ryan dusted the knees of his trousers and headed in the opposite direction. They'd passed *The Sweetheart Clarion* on their walk. He cut through the next alley, hoping to come out in front of the newspaper office. His reckoning was a little off. One block to go. He cast a wary eye behind him and hurried down the street, expecting to hear an angry female roar.

Ryan slipped inside the building. The cheerful bell above his head rang as the door closed. A long counter spanned the front with no one behind it. In the corner of the room sat a desk where a man in his forties with thinning red hair typed at a computer.

Messy stacks of paper covered every surface except for the ones inhabited by empty takeout containers and disposable coffee cups.

"Are you the editor?"

"Yes." He answered without looking up. "Abe Kaiser. How can I help you?"

"Has Katherine Bruno been here?"

"Why?" His gaze jerked to the door. "Is she coming?" Kaiser crouched like he was about to hide under his desk.

"Not that I'm aware. I assumed she might ask the paper to endorse Lanette Johnson since Ms. Bruno's working as her campaign manager."

"Oh, good." His body relaxed. "I'm glad she found another job. I hated letting her go. And not because of her temper."

Ryan rested his arms on the counter. "She worked here?"

"You couldn't find a better employee." Kaiser rose and joined him at the front. "Honest. Dependable. But her pieces always leaned toward an op-ed, no matter what subject I gave her. High school football game? Katie wrote about the inadequate parking. Sweetheart's annual Christmas carol sing-a-long? She pointed out how the tenor section drowned out all the other parts. Everything's a crusade with her."

"I've noticed she has a strong sense of justice."

The man snorted. "What a polite way of putting it."

He extended a hand. "Allow me to introduce myself. I'm—"

"Ryan Park. The political consultant Mayor Johnson imported from New York." Kaiser gave his hand a quick shake.

Ryan nodded. "A good newspaperman always has his finger on the pulse of the city."

"Wish I could claim the credit." The editor grabbed a nearby coffee cup, sniffed its contents, and took a drink. "The truth is, everyone from the minister to the cashier at the quick mart knows about you. It's how small towns work."

"How does it work for convincing you to endorse Harry Johnson's mayoral campaign?"

Kaiser drummed his fingers against the counter. "Endorsement, huh? I took over this place from my dad, and this is the first time anyone's asked for one. Not sure how it works."

"You've never given an endorsement?"

"Never needed to. Harry was the only one who ever ran. 'Til now." His fingers stilled. "I can't believe Lanette is running against her own husband."

"Mayor Johnson put sixteen years of sweat and heart into this town. I'm sure you'll want to ensure his solid leadership continues by endor—"

The bell jangled again.

"There you are."

Ryan's lids shut at the sound of Katherine's voice. Time for misdirection. He turned with a puzzled look. "What happened to you?"

"What happened to me?" She nodded at the man behind him. "Hey, Abe."

Ryan steered her away from the editor. "Better keep up. I've been chatting with Mr. Kaiser here, but I'm ready to leave. How about we talk to voters at the local supermarket? Did I mention how nice your outfit is? Very professional." He half-led, half-pushed her through the doorway and turned. "I'll see you next time, Mr. Kaiser. Please consider my proposal."

The Texas sunlight blinded him as he exited. Ryan withdrew a pair of sunglasses from his pocket and slipped them on. They pulled double-duty as they hid his eyes from the suspicious Katherine. She studied him, her lips pursed.

Ryan grinned. "Ready?"

An uncomfortable three seconds ticked by.

She raised an eyebrow. "Obviously not. But I'll get there."

Chapter Seven

Drums and a driving guitar riff jolted Katherine from her sleep. She sat straight up in bed. Her bleary eyes scanned the darkness. The puppies howled from the other room.

Noise!

Where?

Her brain flickered.

Oh, right. Her ringtone. She'd never heard it at—Katherine glanced at her clock—4:30 in the morning. She grabbed at the lighted screen on her dresser, missed, and knocked a book on the floor. She tried again.

Success!

Katherine pressed the screen and held the phone to her ear.

"Hello?" Her voice sounded an octave lower before dawn.

"Katie? Are you awake?" Somehow Lanette sounded the same—strident as ever.

"Yes."

"Oh, good. Get dressed quick. I'll be by to get you in ten minutes."

"What?" One-word answers were all she could manage before a cup of coffee. "Why?"

"We're going to Dallas. I've made an appointment with the

best photographer in the state, but he only had one slot left. Nine o'clock this morning. I hope the preacher forgives us for skipping church. If we hit the road now, I'll still have time to primp."

Katherine pressed the speaker button, dropped the phone on her bed, and slumped against the headboard. "What do you need pictures for?"

"How can you ask after yesterday?" The slam of a car door carried through the speaker. "The whole town saw me at my worst. Major action is required to wipe that vile memory from their brains pronto. You now have nine minutes to get ready. I'm on my way."

The line went dead. Katherine stared at the screen until the light turned off. She flopped on her pillow, tugged the covers to her chin, and groaned. Why did she take this job?

Tiny yips sounded from the kitchen. Oh, no. The puppies!

She could fill their food and water bowls, but who knew what time she'd return from Dallas? If she left them alone the entire day, she'd have a yellow puddle the size of Lake Amistad when she returned. Who could she ask to dog-sit?

~

Ding-dong.

Ryan cracked one eye open. The bright red numbers of his alarm clock shone in the darkness.

4:35.

Moving to the country was supposed to help him get some rest. Who was at his door before the sun was even up?

Ding-dong. Ding-dong.

Someone persistent. Suspicion hit him as he threw off the comforter and stood. Was this his overbearing next-door neighbor? He ran a hand through his tousled hair and yanked the wrinkled hem of his T-shirt over his sweatpants. Good enough.

Ding-dong. Ding-dong. Ding-dong.

"Hang on!"

Ryan slipped his feet in a pair of slippers and scuffed through the living room to the front door. Grasping the handle, he opened it to find Katherine on his welcome mat, a messy ponytail sticking from the side of her head, holding a large bag.

He sagged against the frame. "How did I know it was you?"

"No time to talk." She passed him the package and raced to her apartment.

Ryan leaned out the door and watched her disappear. He looked at the heavy burden in his arms. The glow of the moonlight illuminated a dog food name. He dropped it on the porch. What was she planning this time?

Katherine reappeared in seconds with her arms full of puppies. "I need a huge favor."

The furry Yorkies squirmed and yipped and struggled for freedom as she walked his way.

Ryan backed up. "You can't be serious."

"I'm sorry. I realize this is asking a lot, but Lanette drafted me to drive her to Dallas, and I can't leave them in their crate all day without a bathroom break. It's too cruel." She tried to walk around him into his place.

He blocked her way. "Don't you have friends? Leave them with Deanna."

"She lives with her mother." Katherine scowled. "Mrs. Day won't let a fly in her spotless house, let alone two dogs. Which leaves my good friend and neighbor, Ryan Park."

"Since when are we friends?" His arms lowered.

"Since now." She passed over the puppies.

He grabbed them by instinct. "Hold it. I'm not a pet person. I refuse to—" The smaller one slipped, and he raised his left leg to try and prop it up.

"Thanks, Ryan." Katherine pulled a ball cap from her pocket and tugged it low on her head. "I owe you one."

She was gone before he could answer.

A whine sounded, and he stared down into two pairs of wide, expectant eyes.

"Yes?"

Another whine.

"What is it? I have zero experience caring for dogs, so you'll have to spell it out for me. Do you want food? Water? A bathroom break?"

Ten hours later, he'd exhausted those options and more. Guarding two puppies was worse than babysitting an infant. They dashed through his house, howled at the slightest noise, and chewed holes in his favorite slippers.

Ryan eventually took refuge on the porch, where there was less furniture for them to destroy. The stiff wicker loveseat pressed into his spine as he collapsed. The breezy summer afternoon might have been pleasant if it weren't for the two hairy charges Katherine had foisted on him. He ignored Romeo and Bella tripping over his feet. Checking his phone, he read a text from the main office in New York. They wanted him to wrap everything up as soon as possible.

"Small potatoes?" He grunted. "Easy for you to say from a thousand miles away."

How did he make his boss understand Sweetheart possessed a myriad of challenges every bit as difficult as a big city campaign?

Romeo jumped into his lap with a whine. Or was it Bella? He checked the dog collar. Pink.

"What?" Ryan stared at her. "You can't be hungry. I already fed you."

She whimpered again.

"Your water bowl is over there." He pointed at the spot by the door.

Bella nudged his hand with her tiny wet nose. Ryan laughed and patted her on the head. "Are you feeling neglected?"

She squirmed closer and made herself comfortable on his lap.

"Just like a woman. Never satisfied." Ryan stroked her downy fur.

Romeo barked as he clawed at the wicker seat near Ryan's leg.

"What's the matter? Your sister made it on her own." He hesitated a second, bent over, and picked him up.

The puppy settled next to Bella. Ryan laid his phone on the seat and rubbed their silky black heads. His breath slowed, and thoughts of the New York office drained from his mind. He sank back and listened to the birds twittering in a nearby oak tree.

Something was missing. What was it?

Traffic.

He couldn't remember the last time he'd been anywhere without the distant roar of cars speeding along the interstate. Now that it was gone, he realized how much he hated the constant drone. If only every day was as peaceful as this one. Bella shifted. Her tiny paws barely registered as she crawled on his chest. He patted her body with soft strokes.

Contentment washed over his spirit as a breeze rustled the tree branches. The leaves brushed together in a whispery lullaby as dreams of strategy meetings, twelve-lane freeways, and a pushy brunette with glinting green eyes wafted through his brain.

Honk-honk.

He jolted. Bella toppled on her brother. They hopped from the chair, howled, and chased each other in a circle.

A large white SUV pulled into the driveway with Lanette Johnson at the wheel. She waved out the open window.

"Son, you're too young to take naps in the middle of the day." She nodded at Katherine in the passenger seat. "Katie insisted we rush home and rescue you from the dogs. You look all right to me, but make her buy you dinner anyway."

Ryan sighed. Dinner with Katherine Bruno. Was that a reward or a punishment?

Chapter Eight

Checkerboard floor tiles reflected the afternoon sunlight shining through the window of The Brunch Café. The popular hangout crackled with life. Hungry customers sat on cherry-red padded stools along the lunch counter, and good-natured chatter filled the room.

Katherine and Ryan took an empty table in the corner and studied their laminated menus.

"Order whatever appeals to you." She placed a cloth napkin in her lap. "Dinner's on me."

Ryan plucked a shiny dog hair from his white T-shirt. "Who has dinner at three o'clock in the afternoon?"

Katherine's lips twitched as the cranky man across from her took a sip of his water. "This place closes early. Thus it's moniker The Brunch Café. Susanna Sheppard, the owner, isn't much of a night owl."

He'd been growling ever since they woke him on the front porch, cuddled with the two puppies. Was he embarrassed to be caught in a sensitive light?

"Don't ever ask me to watch those mutts again." Ryan tugged at the collar of his shirt.

Definitely embarrassed.

Katherine tamped down the desire to laugh. "It was an emergency."

"Since when are glamour shots an emergency?" He crossed his arms over his chest.

"Lanette is very—" Katherine was proud of herself for censoring the first word which came to mind. "Lanette is very image conscious." So much kinder than calling someone vain. "You can imagine how horrified she was when the whole town saw her at her worst."

"Did you find out who posted the pictures?"

Katherine raised an eyebrow. "I'm still not a hundred percent convinced it wasn't you."

His chair legs grated against the floor as he shoved away from the table.

"I'm sorry." Katherine reached out a hand. "You did me a favor. I shouldn't be so suspicious. But other than the mayoral race, why would anyone want to humiliate Lanette? She's an acquired taste, but we love her."

Susanna Sheppard approached with a round tray. "Be careful." She placed a saucer of butter and a basket of yeast rolls between them. "These are fresh out of the oven."

The diamond in Susanna's wedding ring flashed under Katherine's nose as she set the food down.

"How's married life?" Katherine smiled.

After a whirlwind courtship, Susanna had married her childhood best friend, Daniel, and set the gossips' tongues wagging.

"It's cozy." The twinkle in her eye said more than her words. "I hope you find out for yourself soon."

"From your mouth to God's ear. But in the meantime, I'd like to talk about your security camera outside the restaurant." Katherine bent forward with both elbows on the table. "I forgot you installed one. Would you check the footage for me?"

Ryan plucked a roll from the basket and slid the butter dish closer. "Do you think it caught the person who taped Lanette's pictures around town?"

Susanna winced. "I saw those. Someone left a few on the café window."

Katherine shot up and tossed her napkin on the table. "Can I look at the footage? I'd love to catch the creep."

"Sorry. A bird flew into my outside camera the other day, and it's on the fritz. My husband's the one with the technical know-how, and he's been too busy to fix it."

"Figures." Katherine sank to her chair. "It couldn't be that easy."

Susanna patted her back and headed for a customer waving a coffee mug in the air.

"Good evening, Katie." Her next-door neighbor, Betty Gannett, stopped at their table. Still in her church clothes, she wore purple lace from head to toe. The woman's short, curly hairdo vibrated as her attention swung from Ryan to Katherine.

"Hi, Mrs. Gannett. Have you met Ryan Park, the mayor's campaign manager?" Katherine tipped her head. "Ryan, this is Betty Gannett, our town clerk."

He stood and offered her his hand. "A pleasure to meet you."

The woman beamed at the handsome stranger as he greeted her.

Ryan returned to his seat, and Mrs. Gannett clasped her fingers together. "I heard Katie was working for Lanette's campaign. Doesn't that make you two rivals? Nice to see you can still eat dinner together."

Katherine grabbed her neighbor's lacy sleeve. "I'm glad you stopped by. I need volunteers for our street team. Care to join the winning side?"

"Oh," the woman blinked twice, "I ... I don't know too much about politics."

"It doesn't matter. You know Lanette."

"More than I care to." Mrs. Gannett's mouth puckered as if she ate a slice of sour lemon. "The truth is, she and I don't get along too well ever since she talked me into sitting in the dunking booth at the auxiliary's annual fundraiser. Lanette Johnson passes off her dirty work like nobody's business."

Katherine let go of the woman's sleeve. Would she have to run the campaign single-handed? Deanna liked her Uncle Harry too much. Mrs. Gannett liked Lanette too little. How many excuses would she hear before this was over?

"You understand." Mrs. Gannett gave a tentative smile. "Don't you, Katie?"

"Huh?" She understood too well. "Sure."

Her neighbor's lower lip poked out. Katherine stared. Was she supposed to make Mrs. Gannett feel better about refusing? Shouldn't it be the other way around?"

Ryan cleared his throat and motioned to the woman's outfit. "What a lovely lace jacket."

She blushed and giggled in a way that didn't match her age. "I dieted for two months to fit into it. Every night, I dreamed of ice cream sundaes. It's been the most miserable forty-five days of my life."

Katherine's gaze met Ryan's. He covered his mouth with a napkin.

Her brows lowered. "Forty-five days isn't—"

Ryan laid his hand on hers. Her words stuttered to a stop. Was his body always this warm? His fingers felt like lean, muscular branding irons. What were they talking about? Oh, right, sundaes. And her neighbor's inability to count.

He gave her a slight shake of his head and grinned at Mrs. Gannett. "The hardest part is always the beginning. I'm sure the next two months will fly by."

Katherine mumbled, "If the first two ever finish."

His foot jabbed hers under the table, and she grimaced. Why did Ryan insist on encouraging the futile ambitions of Mrs. Gannett's diet? Was he bucking for another voter?

"I hope you're right." Mrs. Gannett's cheeks glowed. "I'll stop interrupting the young people's evening repast. Enjoy."

Katherine glared at Ryan as he waved goodbye. She waited until Mrs. Gannett was out of earshot, then gave him an answering kick.

"Ow!" He stooped and rubbed his foot. "Was that really necessary?"

"Who are you to shush me like a five-year-old child?"

"You were about to jump in and spoil her story."

She slapped the table. "Forty-five days isn't two months."

"Not in so many words."

"Not in *any* words. It's a month and a half."

"What good would it do to correct the math?" He took his knife, cut open a dinner roll, and slathered butter across the fluffy inside.

Katherine opened her mouth and closed it again. She shrugged. "Probably none."

"Exactly. Why ruin her mood by being blunt?"

"I'm not blunt. I'm honest."

"As well I know." He laughed. "Believe it or not, I find your honesty charming."

Fire streaked across her cheeks. No one had ever found anything about her charming, let alone her tendency to tell it straight. Katherine grabbed her water glass and took a long drink. The icy liquid cooled her body and provided an opportunity to decompress.

Ryan eyed her. "But have you ever considered the difference between honesty and being harsh?"

Katherine sputtered. Her teeth clenched, and she clunked the glass on the table. She went from charming to harsh in five seconds. So much for feeling flattered.

He made it sound easy. Just hold her tongue. If it were simple, she would have done it years ago. The three weeks she'd sweetened her speech like a honeycomb had almost been the death of her.

She gave a tight-lipped smile. "What can I say? I guess my mean streak runs too deep."

"That's not meanness." He folded his arms on the table and leaned forward. "It's passion. I don't think anyone in this town realizes how much you care and how hard you work to show it. It's not your fault you struggle with communicating."

A fluttery gasp escaped her lips. The temperature in her body rose and burned the back of her eyeballs. She batted her lashes, willing the gusher of pent-up tears to stay put. Crying was for losers.

Katherine cleared her throat. Twice. She managed a defiant glance and found Ryan focused on his piece of bread, applying a second coat to the already well-buttered roll.

RYAN SUSPECTED Katherine Bruno didn't break down often and wouldn't appreciate him witnessing her moment of weakness. But smoothing over awkward situations was his specialty. He took his time with the bread, and when he looked up, she was composed.

He smiled. "How are you adjusting to the role of campaign manager?"

A wary expression crossed her face. "Why?"

Ryan set his knife on the plate. "Personal experience has taught me what a burden it can be."

"Burden?" She laughed as she pressed both hands over her heart. "Great description. My spirit is toting a knapsack filled with rocks everywhere I go."

"Then why do it?" He asked without an ulterior motive. Correction. Only a slight motive. He was in politics, after all, and his job would be much easier if Katherine quit the campaign. But mostly, he wanted to know why she endured the endless stream of requests from her pushy candidate.

"Some burdens are worth the weight." She removed her hands from her chest, clutched them into fists, and pushed them against the table. "And if anyone tries to stop Lanette or embarrass her again, they'll have to get through me first."

The stubborn set of her soft pink lips told him she meant every word. One delicate brow arched higher than the other, daring him to try. His stomach bounced as he gave a silent chuckle. Safer to change the subject.

"How goes the search for volunteers?"

She unclenched her fists and spread her napkin in her lap. It was hard to believe she was close to breaking down a minute ago. No trace of her earlier distress remained.

"Not as well as I'd expected. I assumed Lanette's army of auxiliary minions would jump to help her, but people feel guilty working against the mayor."

"Understandable." He took a bite of the roll. The light, buttery goodness melted against his tongue in a savory testament to the power of home-cooking. "Sixteen years in office builds a lot of loyalty."

"What can I do?"

"Asking for advice? You do realize we're on opposite sides in this battle?"

"It's hard to forget."

He shouldn't help her, but what did it matter? He'd done his research, and if everything went according to plan, Lanette's campaign would be finished by midnight tomorrow, and he'd book a flight to New York. Far away from fiery office mates with hair-trigger tempers.

"What can I do?" she repeated.

Ryan smirked. "Pay them."

"No money."

He downed a sip of water. "Then I suggest the guilt trip method. Find anyone who owes you anything and call in the favor."

"A favor? That's more in my wheelhouse." Katherine grabbed a piece of bread from the basket. "Putting a leash on my tongue is impossible," she tore the roll in half and grinned, "but I can do guilt."

Ryan raised his glass to her in a toast. "Godspeed."

His lips quivered as he took another drink. He pitied the poor soul Katherine had in mind. Whoever it was didn't stand a chance.

Chapter Nine

The Monday morning sunlight streamed through the campaign office window as Deanna Day plopped on the striped couch and curled her feet under her navy-blue sundress.

"There must be an expiration date on favors." She smoothed her pompadour hairstyle. "How can you call in a debt from tenth grade?"

"Let me remind you," Katherine set a bag of baked goodies from The Brunch Café on the coffee table, "the teacher gave me detention for passing those notes, and I still didn't rat you out the love poem was yours, not mine."

Deanna's fingers stilled. Several seconds passed before she sighed. "Evan Colter. He had the bluest eyes." She peeked in the bag and perused the selection of muffins and cookies. Picking up the teapot, she raised a dainty cup and saucer. "At least you brought decent refreshments."

"Oh, my lands!" Lanette hollered from the front door. "Deanna, I knew you'd support me, precious child."

Elise poked her chubby face over Lanette's shoulder. "I'm glad to see there's some loyalty left. I talked to half the town at church on Sunday and couldn't get anyone to come help us."

"You want loyalty, Aunt Lanette?" Deanna poked two thumbs at her chest. "I'm your gal."

The older women settled in the brocade chairs and helped themselves to the tea.

Katherine downed two blueberry streusel muffins in a row and wiped the crumbs from her mouth. "The first order of business is to choose a campaign treasurer to supervise the money."

"Leave it to me." Lanette broke a lemon crinkle cookie in two. "I don't mind bookkeeping."

Katherine shook her head. "It's bad ethics for the candidate to be in charge of their own funds."

"Oooh!" Elise raised her hand. "Can I do it?"

Lanette nodded. "You'd be perfect. You know how to pinch a penny until Lincoln yelps. I hereby appoint you my official campaign treasurer."

"I get a title and everything." Elise glowed. "What does a campaign treasurer do?"

"How should I know? Ask my manager."

Katherine took a calming breath. "You'll keep track of any money we raise and be sure to collect the receipts for our purchases. I assume there are tax forms we'll have to fill out."

Elise pulled a small brown notebook from her purse and grabbed a pen from the table. "Keep track of money. Collect receipts. Research tax forms."

A masculine voice sounded outside the door. Ryan entered, talking on his cell phone. "Yes. It won't be long. Yes."

He gave a friendly wave to the group and sat at his desk.

"Welcome, Mr. Park." Elise dropped her notebook in her lap and grasped her teacup. She took a sip of the dark brew and grimaced. "Katie, your tea resembles your personality."

Katherine gripped the back of a chair. "Strong?"

"Hard to take." Elise choked as she set her drink on the coffee table. "What's my first duty as campaign treasurer?"

Katherine pushed an angry retort down her throat. As the

manager, she must behave in a professional manner, even if her volunteers made personal remarks. "You can brainstorm fundraiser ideas."

"What for?" Deanna swung her legs off the couch and adjusted her skirt with a ladylike swish. "Can't we just talk to everyone we know?"

Katherine's gaze darted to Ryan. Had he heard? The glimmer of a smile appeared, but he turned away and kept talking on his phone as he grabbed a paper from his desk drawer.

It was humiliating, placing their ignorance on full display. And she was the most ignorant of all. How could they run a successful campaign when she had no idea what she was doing? Forget sleep for the foreseeable future. Her nights would be spent reading and researching this unfamiliar political world.

"Word of mouth is a great tactic," she nodded at Deanna, "but we need posters, handbills, mailouts. The works."

Lanette popped the last bit of cookie in her mouth. "Spare no expense."

Elise whistled. "Sounds expensive."

Katherine looked again at her opponent across the room, but he was focused on the paper. His lips curled upward, and he heaved a satisfied sigh. What had caused such an expression? She stood, wandered over, and glimpsed a list.

Ryan pressed his cell between his shoulder and his ear and slipped the paper into a large manila envelope. "Yes, Amy." He grabbed hold of the phone again. "Can't someone else wrangle Mr. Benson?" He headed for the exit. "I understand. I should return within a week. If he chooses to make an appointment, I'll see him then."

A muggy gust of air entered the office as the door opened and closed behind him.

"Did you hear what he said?" Katherine hurried to the window and studied Ryan as he walked to his car.

"He mentioned an appointment." Deanna paused. "Is that significant?"

"Ryan said he'd see them in a week. It's June. The election isn't until August."

"What's the matter, Katie?" Elise snickered. "Afraid you'll miss him?"

Katherine paced between the window and the couch. Her gut told her there was more to the story. But what? She paused and tapped a finger against a lacy throw pillow. "Something's off."

"How so?" Elise seized the sugar bowl and transferred three helpings to her teacup. Her spoon clinked against the porcelain as she stirred.

Katherine returned to the window and stared at Ryan's tall figure in the distance. "He's too confident."

Lanette scowled. "He thinks he can run circles around us with his big city know-how."

"No. There's more. A look in his eye. Like he has all four aces in his hand."

"And a couple up his sleeve." Her boss sniffed. "Anyone who chooses politics as his vocation can't be trusted."

Elise smirked. "Does that include Harry?"

"Not in a million years. My husband is the exception. He serves this town out of the goodness of his heart."

"Couldn't be 'cause he appreciates everyone polishing his apple?"

"Apples don't pay the bills. In sixteen years, he hasn't taken a salary once. He's probably lost money with the hours he's spent on town business. Even with my help, the mountain of paperwork grows quicker than a fire ant hill."

"Paperwork," Katherine muttered.

The memory of Ryan shoving a list of signatures into the manila envelope floated through her brain. He'd never been without a clipboard this week. She'd assumed he was recruiting volunteers for the mayor's campaign. Was she missing an important detail?

She dug her phone out of her purse and called up the search engine. Hitting the microphone emblem, she held the speaker to her mouth. "What do I need to do to become mayor?"

Elise staggered to her feet. A splotch of tea swished from her cup and splashed on the rug. "You're running for mayor too?"

"Don't be ridiculous. Who'd elect me?" Katherine scrolled through the list of results on her screen and clicked a link. "Things to do before running for office," she read aloud. "Check your eligibility. Gather support staff. Turn in your petition of candidacy before the deadline."

"Your what?" Deanna's head turned sideways like a puppy in a pet store window.

Katherine typed frantically into her phone. Her stomach sank as she read the results. "A candidate must obtain signatures from at least four percent of the number of voters who participated in the last election in order to qualify for a political ballot. The deadline to turn in your petition is the eighth Tuesday before voting day."

She dashed to the calendar by Ryan's desk and flipped to August. Moving backward through the months, she counted the number of Tuesdays from the election.

"Six, Seven, Eight." Her finger landed on the date with the red circle around it. "Today. Why that no good weasel."

"What is it?" Lanette thunked her cup on the table and stood. "Is something wrong?"

"How many people voted the last time your husband was elected?"

"I can tell you exactly. He got seven hundred seventy-seven votes." She rolled her eyes. "Harry had seriously considered not running again. But, when he saw the results, he said the number was a sign from Heaven it was meant to be."

"Seven hundred seventy-seven." Katherine tried to do the math in her head. "Four percent of seven hundred seventy-seven is ... aargh." The pressure made even simple calculations impossible as her brain whizzed from one thought to the next. She opened the calculator on her phone and typed in the numbers. "Thirty-one point zero eight. We'd better round up to be safe."

"Am I the only one not following this conversation?" Elise said around a mouthful of shortbread.

"Drop the cookies." Katherine grabbed her candidate by the French-tipped fingers. "We have to get a petition from the town clerk, find thirty-two signatures, and turn it in by five o'clock this afternoon."

∾

RYAN CHECKED his watch and smirked.

4:55 p.m.

Without another official candidate on the ballot, he could finish this job and return to New York in a matter of days. A slight twinge of regret hit him. The quaint ambiance of Sweetheart must have wormed its way into his affections. He'd expected to find the smallness boring. The people unvaried and cloying. He hadn't expected to feel invigorated.

Was it the quirky but charming locals? The restful peace that was impossible to find in his normal hectic lifestyle? Maybe the fiery, unfiltered brunette who always kept him guessing?

Yes. Katherine was the biggest surprise he'd found in Sweetheart.

Smart. Passionate. Attractive—in an unrefined way.

Too bad she'd refuse to speak to him after today.

He checked his watch again.

4:58 p.m.

Betty Gannett turned off her antiquated computer monitor, removed her town clerk nametag, and pulled her purse from a desk drawer. "Can I help you with anything else, Ryan?"

"No, Betty." He rose from the bench. "Thanks for letting me kill time here. I've got to meet the mayor for dinner."

"Tell Harry I said hello."

"Will do." Ryan crossed the small waiting area and reached

for the door handle. It bumped his knuckles as it opened from the outside.

Katherine strode into the office without sparing him a glance. Her shoes made an angry *slap-slap* against the linoleum floor. She smacked a paper on the counter and thumped her fist on top. "Thanks for faxing me the form, Mrs. Gannett. Thirty-two signatures exactly."

Betty checked the clock on the wall. "Didn't think you were coming, Katie. I was about to head on home."

Ryan bit down a groan. How did Katherine figure it out? He'd avoided discussing it with Mayor Johnson for fear the man might let something slip to his wife.

The door crashed open again, hitting Ryan between the shoulder blades. Two bodies careened past him as Lanette and Elise barreled into the office. They skidded to a stop in front of the counter.

"Did we," Lanette clutched her heaving bosom, "make it," she gasped, "in time?"

"Barely." Betty tilted her nose at Lanette, perused the document, and nodded. "Looks okay. You have the required number of signatures. Just one requirement left to check off."

Ryan ground his teeth and pulled out his phone. Better text the company and tell them he wouldn't return as soon as he'd hoped. Katherine swung his way with a scowl. She probably wanted to stick her tongue out at him. A justifiable reaction.

Betty withdrew a paper from her file cabinet and grabbed a pen. "I have to ask you a few questions. If you get the correct answers, your candidacy is official."

Elise's jaw dropped. "She has to take a test?"

A hysterical bubble of laughter welled in Ryan's throat. How could this trio of small-town clowns keep blocking him at every turn?

"Nooooooo," Betty drawled. "She doesn't take a test."

Lanette fanned herself. "Oh, thank Heaven. I always choked on tests in school."

"Let me see." Betty's pen hovered over the document. "First question. Do you have a high school diploma?"

"Of course, I have a diploma." Lanette huffed. "I did poorly on tests, but I wasn't *that* bad."

"Second question. Do you have a residence in the town of Sweetheart?"

"You were there on Saturday for the beauty pageant committee meeting. Did you forget already?"

"No sarcasm, please." Betty checked another item off the paper. "Third question. Are you over the age of eighteen?"

"Mrs. Gannett, please." Katherine pushed a long strand of hair behind her ear. The once tidy ponytail had turned into a mass of frizzies. "It's been a long day."

"Over eighteen," Betty muttered. She studied the list, checked items off, and dropped her pen in a cup. "Lanette Johnson, you meet the requirements to have your name on the mayoral ballot for the town of Sweetheart. Congratulations, and Heaven help us all if you win."

Lanette thumped her palm on the counter. "Save your congratulations for election night," she spun around and pointed her French-tipped finger at Ryan, "when we're going to make this good-lookin' boy cry."

Elise stepped behind her, poked her chin out, and nodded.

Ryan ducked his head and willed his lips to remain still. It wouldn't do to laugh in their faces. This registration setback was a mere bump in the road. These women had no idea the countless hours of work and stress a successful campaign required. Let them experience a true taste of politics and see who stuck around.

The click of high heels passed him, but he kept his gaze trained on the floor. The outside door slammed shut. He chuckled. The tips of two white canvas shoes entered his field of vision. He manufactured a blank expression and looked up a pair of long, jean-clad legs, past a half-tucked T-shirt, and into the eyes of Katherine Bruno.

Were those lightning bolts flashing in the green orbs?

Her breaths came short and quick as she stared him down.

Ryan cleared his throat and smiled. "Cutting it kind of close with the paperwork. You got here in the nick of time."

"No thanks to you." She spit the words out.

"Why would I assist my competition with anything? Even in congenial Sweetheart, there must be a limit."

"Common decency?" She crowded in. "I guess that was expecting too much from someone like you. I thought I glimpsed a human being in the last few days, but you were biding your time—waiting for me to make a fool of myself." Her volume rose. "If you can't beat a backwater hick like me without dirty tricks, I wonder why Mayor Johnson bothered to import a political consultant from New York. He could have found any number of cheaper, less-crooked options on the internet."

"Crooked?" Ryan bent forward until they were level, his face an inch from hers. "There's nothing dishonest about doing my job and ensuring my worthy client has every advantage he deserves. I work for Mayor Johnson, not his wife. She's your problem."

"You're my problem!" Katherine shouted so hard a trace of spit hit his cheek.

He stood tall and wiped the moisture away. "Consider this fair warning. I've never lost a campaign, and I'm not starting in Sweetheart, Texas. Don't ask me for advice or follow me around. We're on opposite sides of this battlefield, and I fight clean but hard. You're on your own."

So much for the flirtation strategy. He'd just declared war.

Chapter Ten

C itizens of Sweetheart poured into the community center in a talkative, enthusiastic herd. Mayor Johnson's first political rally was the place to be on a Saturday night. After many weeks in town, Ryan knew most of them by name. He stood by the door and offered whatever kind of greeting fit each particular voter's personality.

"Good evening, Mrs. Thibodeaux. I love the hat."

The minister's wife tilted the flower-bedecked boater and beamed at him.

"Hey, partner." Ryan waved at Wilbur Lansing as he entered the double doors. "How about that game the other night?"

Wilbur screwed up his nose. "Not worth the time it took to watch."

Ryan nodded, not sure which sport they were talking about. He noted a few metal folding chairs remained open. They should fill up in no time. He'd tried to estimate how many people would attend and purposefully had his team put out a smaller number. Adding chairs at the last minute gave the impression of a hot-ticket event.

He'd also chosen the community center for a specific purpose. It highlighted the need for a new meeting place if there was standing-room only at the event. When Mayor Johnson presented the plans for the proposed town hall, the contrast between the outdated wood paneling and well-worn linoleum floors would be evident.

The temperature rose as bodies packed the room. Ryan fanned his black button-down shirt as he checked his watch. Five minutes to go. Better make sure the refreshment table was stocked.

Mayor Johnson stood by the water bottles chatting with Jud Watson as Ryan approached.

"Excuse me, Mayor." He nodded at the men. "It's almost time to start."

"Hello, Ry." Jud slapped him on the back. "Glad you're gathering the town to support my boy, Harry."

"We want the best for Mayor Johnson."

"He deserves it." Jud jerked a thumb at his friend. "After he gets done building our fancy town hall, they'll erect a statue of him in the lobby."

Ryan cocked his head. "You've heard? We tried to keep it under wraps until the big announcement."

Mayor Johnson laughed. "There's no such thing as a secret in Sweetheart, son. I bet half the people in this room already know."

"Besides," Jud threw his arm around the mayor's shoulders, "it's kind of hard to keep me in the dark. They're building on my land. I gave the town a huge discount. More than one oil company offered big money for the rights to drill, but it's a small price to pay if it helps my buddy out. We go back a long way. Don't we, Harry?"

"First grade." The mayor nodded. "I'm not sure why we didn't attend Kindergarten together."

"I think I was so smart I skipped a grade." Jud chuckled. "But in all those years, have you ever known me to lead you astray?"

Ryan's inner cynic raised an eyebrow. The garrulous rancher

was working every emotional trick in the book. Better than many he'd seen in the big political arenas. Jud Watson plucked that loyal heartstring of Harry Johnson's like a pro.

The mayor jabbed his friend in the gut. "Don't talk crazy. You've pulled my fat from the fire too many times to count."

"Ow!" Jud grabbed his side and coughed. "I suppose we're getting too old to roughhouse." He snatched a bottle of water from the table.

Mayor Johnson studied the refreshments. "When are you bringing out the rest of the food?"

"The rest?" Ryan surveyed the spread of candy mints and branded water bottles with Harry Johnson's picture. "I hadn't—"

Jud slammed his bottle on the table. "You gotta be kidding me. What's she doing here?"

Ryan followed Jud's angry glare to Katherine Bruno walking through the double doors. She wore a gray T-shirt with a blue cardigan, jeans, and her purse strapped across her body. Her thick brown hair was gathered in the usual ponytail.

He turned to Jud. "I hope she came to her senses and decided to support Mayor Johnson."

Jud guffawed and slapped him on the same spot as before. Ryan bid goodbye to the men and rolled his aching spine as he walked away.

What was she doing here?

The principled Katherine would never desert Lanette in a million years. If he had learned one thing in the past month, it was the integrity of his opposition. She could outwork, outpace, and out-yell half the political consultants in New York. She was no pushover.

After his tactical omission about the certificate of candidacy, there might as well have been a line of demarcation drawn in their shared office. Small talk and socializing were non-existent. Not that he minded. He preferred strictly business. She kept to her side and filled her rosebud-painted desk to overflowing with stacks of paper, signs, and whatever other junk she needed, while he steered clear of the mess and its maddening creator.

Katherine spotted him and gave the curtest of nods before taking an empty chair in the last row.

Ryan shook his head. Too bad a bulldog like that wasn't on his side. He predicted tonight's rally would be a huge blow to their adversary's campaign. Everything was top-notch, from the tri-fold brochures to the three-minute commercial playing on the large screen. Time to introduce Podunk to the big dreams their mayor had in store.

KATHERINE SQUIRMED in her metal chair as Mayor Johnson gave his speech. Was it in bad taste to attend the opposition's rally? She'd honestly wanted to hear more about the building project. Despite her new job title, Sweetheart was still her home. She observed the enraptured audience. They were eating up the new town hall faster than a hot fudge sundae with double sprinkles.

Mayor Johnson waved at the virtual rendering on the screen. "And this beautiful town hall will be a place that serves you, your children, and generations down the road."

Applause exploded around Katherine. She was forced to admit the mockups were impressive. Full-color drawings from the architect showed a two-story building with Corinthian columns on the front and attached wings on either side to house the new sheriff's department and meeting rooms. It was more of a complex than a town hall.

Katherine looked to the back. Ryan stood against the wall with contentment covering his face, no doubt enjoying the crowd's exuberant response. Gasps of surprised delight had peppered the presentation.

Mayor Johnson basked in the glow of the audience's approval. His chest puffed out, and he took the microphone from the stand to walk in front of the people.

"Does anyone have any questions?"

Willy Walker raised a hand in the front row. "How soon will it be done?"

Laughter rippled through the crowd.

The mayor smiled. "The blueprints are ready to go, and the bonds to purchase the land will be available in November. Christmas is coming early this year."

A few listeners clapped and whistled.

Wilbur hollered from the chair in front of Katherine. "How are you holding up with your wife running against you?"

Mayor Johnson's smile wavered. "I admit the situation isn't ideal."

"Let her know who's boss!" an unidentified male voice called.

Katherine glowered in the commenter's direction.

To the mayor's credit, he shot a disapproving glare at whoever had spoken. "My wife is an essential part of what makes this town great."

"She was until she got too big for her britches." Jud raised halfway from his seat. "There's no way she can do half the things you've accomplished. Lanette is great at the decorations and festival stuff, but she should leave the business end to you."

Mayor Johnson twisted his lips and shook his head. "Jud, I appreciate your support, but—"

A woman on the other side popped from her seat. "I support you, too, Harry. Even stopped going to the Ladies Auxiliary. Lanette had no call stabbing you in the back."

Heads nodded, and murmurs of agreement sounded from the crowd.

Mayor Johnson gripped the microphone and waved down as if he could squash the insurrection. "Folks. Please, don't—"

Katherine's temperature rose with all the finesse of an over-packed pressure cooker. She released a breath. Another.

It didn't help.

She shot to her feet. "I won't sit here and listen to a bunch of mealy-mouthed, sloth-footed old geezers tear down Lanette Johnson. Without her, Sweetheart would still be mortgaged to the hilt with most of Main Street boarded up. You offer your opinions easily, but she was the one who led the charge and did something about it. Lanette forced people to get off their duffs and work to make this town a clean, safe place again."

"That's right, girl." Mary Thibodeaux raised an open palm from the front row like she was giving the preacher an amen.

"You're afraid of progress." Jud Watson shoved his cowboy hat back on his head.

"Progress?" Katherine motioned to the screen. "Sweetheart is barely five thousand citizens. This proposed town hall costs more than one built for a population twice our size."

"Katie," Mayor Johnson tugged at the cord of his microphone, "we can pass this on to the next generation. A showpiece for the town."

"Who are we trying to impress?" She swung her arms wide. "I'm sure your children and grandchildren will be much more appreciative of a home that isn't saddled in debt, but you can't see past your over-inflated egos."

Faces hardened, and heads shook as rumbling filled the room. Would she be dragged out by the scruff of her neck? Better hurry and say what she wanted.

Katherine walked to the middle aisle and turned in a circle as she spoke. "Mayor Johnson, I love you, but those of us in this room over the age of twelve remember the hard times. I refuse to return to the days of litter-lined streets when half the people in Sweetheart lived below the poverty level. So, I'm voting for Lanette, and anyone with half a brain better do the same."

She spun and marched to the exit. Boos and insults followed her.

"Someone ought to shut that gal's mouth," a rancher mumbled.

Katherine raised her chin. She caught a glimpse of Ryan

behind the crowd. He stood in the same spot, arms and ankles crossed, with an amused grin. He dipped his head as she passed. Know-it-all.

She'd been in danger of falling for his dog-sitting charms, but he'd revealed his true colors when he tried to trick Lanette out of her chance to run. Who knew what else he was capable of?

"Don't be fooled again," Katherine muttered to herself. "Stay away from the competition."

Chapter Eleven

L ate afternoon sunlight spilled through the office window as Ryan worked on the weekly volunteer schedule. Thanks to Katherine's big speech at the rally, he had five new men offering their time to Mayor Johnson's campaign. It appeared some of the male population felt threatened by a well-spoken woman.

She'd been a sight to behold. Fire and passion exploding from every pore. He hated to admit it, but several of the points she made were valid. Why was the tab for the new town hall so steep in a little town like Sweetheart?

The squeak of the door told him Katherine had returned from lunch. He sat forward and typed, not expecting a greeting. Despite working in the same space and living side by side, their little scuffle over the candidacy petition ended any friendly interactions. In the last month, she'd spoken a mere four words to him. *Leave my dog alone.* If Bella hadn't scampered over when he was out for an evening jog, she wouldn't have said that much.

He'd welcomed the freedom from her tenacious pursuit. At first. But it made for a tense work environment. There must be a way to make their everyday interplay more harmonious. Ryan drummed his fingers against the desk. Perhaps if he made the first move, they could call a truce. He shut the lid of his laptop and spun his chair.

Katherine sat at her desk with an extra-large smoothie cup. She sucked the straw, and the last few drops rattled in the bottom.

He smiled. "I think it's empty."

She crumpled the paper cup and threw it away. Fanning herself with one hand, she shuffled through a pile of flyers with the other.

Okay. *No* to the small talk. Perhaps a sincere compliment.

"You made a salient point at the rally last night."

Two suspicious green eyes swerved in his direction. At least she was looking at him.

He pressed his advantage. "The price tag for the new town hall isn't exactly a bargain. I wonder why it costs so much."

KATHERINE KEPT HER MOUTH CLOSED. If he thought he could worm his way into her good graces by agreeing with her, he'd be disappointed. Still—

She'd had plenty of opportunities to observe him over the last few weeks. He treated every person who came into the office with respect, whether they represented his campaign or hers. She'd never once heard Ryan give unscrupulous instructions to his volunteers, and she worked and lived with him. Correction. Lived beside him. Unless he was meeting them in the woods after midnight, that left no time for him to organize anything underhanded.

He'd infuriated her by hiding the requirement about registering a candidate for the ballot by a certain date. But once she'd calmed down, she admitted to herself she might have done the same thing if the situation were reversed. It wasn't dishonest, just clever. Though she'd die before confessing it to anyone but herself, she liked the guy.

In a professional, platonic way.

Katherine drummed her fingers on top of her desk. "If you find it fishy, why don't you investigate?"

"I didn't say it was fishy. Overpriced would be a better term. It seems someone wasn't good at negotiating a bargain." Ryan motioned to a box of flyers at her feet. "Do you plan to canvas the weekend crowd?"

"Why?"

He bent and pulled a similar box from under his desk. "I was going out in about an hour. Rather than gang up on the same voters, why don't we compromise?"

It sounded reasonable. She'd chased away more than one citizen by shoving in when Ryan was already talking to them.

Katherine scratched the side of her neck. "Should we divide Main Street down the middle?"

Ryan squinted. "You mean each take one side of the road?"

"Yes." It would be a relief to get out of the stuffy office. Was the air conditioning broken? She cleared the phlegm in her throat. "But no switching if I happen to get the busier stretch."

"And how do we choose who gets which side?"

"Flip a coin." She rose from her chair and swayed. Grasping the side of the desk, she rubbed her throat. "Does it feel warm in here to you?"

"No." He stood and stretched out his hand. "You've got a deal."

The sunlight hit his jet-black hair and gave his face an ethereal glow. Katherine felt overheated staring at the gorgeous man in front of her. Had he turned the thermostat up? She moved forward to meet him.

Ryan's eyes widened. "Katherine!" He grabbed her by the elbow.

"What?"

He tugged her to the bathroom, flipped on the light, and stood her in front of the mirror.

"Oh, my word!" Katherine stared at the less-than-gorgeous reflection.

Her cheeks resembled a cartoon chipmunk, almost twice their normal size. She pressed her hands to her swollen skin and examined it. Tiny red spots dotted her neck, and a rosy flush splayed above her T-shirt.

Ryan stood at the threshold. "Is there anything I can do?"

"Yes." She pushed on his broad shoulder. "Get out!"

Katherine slammed the door in his face and leaned her forehead against the wood.

Wouldn't he have a collection of hilarious anecdotes to tell his big-city friends when he returned to New York?

All of them featuring her.

Chapter Twelve

Ryan hovered at the door of the tiny bathroom. He touched the battered wood but hesitated at knocking. His surly officemate hadn't made a peep in five minutes. Was she okay?

"Katherine?" He tapped. "Need any help? Do you want me to call someone?"

"Like who?" Her sarcastic tone carried through the barricade.

"I don't know. The paramedics? A friend? An exorcist?" When she didn't answer, he tried again. "If none of those sound appealing, I'm offering my services. Free of charge."

More silence.

The door opened a crack. He waited, but she didn't emerge.

"Katherine?"

He gave the wood a cautious push. She stood in front of the mirror with her swollen lower lip sticking out, hands braced against the sink. Ryan wasn't sure if her watery eyes were another symptom or if she was close to a breakdown.

He pointed at the spots covering her neck. "Do you have any idea what caused this?"

"It's an allergic reaction." She grabbed a paper towel from the receptacle, ran it under a cold stream of water, and pressed it to her cheek.

"Has it happened before?"

"Yes, but not often. I don't understand. The only thing that makes me break out this way is pineapple."

"What did you eat for lunch?"

"A burger and fries at the café." She dabbed her neck. "And I ordered a smoothie to-go, but it was orange mango."

"Could the person who prepared it have used pineapple by mistake?"

"Impossible. Susanna and I went to school together. She knows I'm allergic, and she'd never make such a careless mistake."

Ryan studied her from head to toe. The red dots multiplied by the minute. Her labored breaths echoed off the bathroom tile.

"Let's take you to the doctor." He led her into the office.

"No!" Katherine's sneakers squeaked against the floor as she dug in her heels. "I have too much to do. I need to pass out those flyers."

"In this condition?" He pointed at her face. "It's rude to say, but you'll scare the children."

She shoved past him, weaving as she walked.

Ryan followed and put a hand on her back to steady her. Katherine's body heat radiated through the thin material. "You go outside, and they'll think you're drunk. The last thing your campaign needs is another scandal."

"It'll wear off." She batted him away. "This isn't my first time. A little dizziness, swelling, a clogged throat. And then it lets up."

He crossed his arms. "How about medicine?"

Katherine sat on the couch. "Antihistamine helps." Propping a throw pillow behind her, she kneaded her temple. "The swelling disappears faster when I take it."

"There's some in my desk." He ran over and slid the drawer out. "I bought it in case the pollen was bad." He opened the box, checked the instructions, and popped the pills from the silver package. "You'd better take the maximum dose."

Ryan pulled a bottle of water from his duffel bag and passed it to her with the medicine.

"Thanks." She swallowed the pills and took a long drink.

"Which brand is it?"

He held up the pink package for her to see.

"Are you crazy?" She thunked the bottle on the coffee table. Water sloshed onto the surface. "Why not feed me a sleeping pill? That stuff makes me pass out for hours."

He turned the box over and read the side effects. "It says it may cause drowsiness, but that's never happened to me."

Katherine scratched her fiery skin. "I've tried every antihistamine on the market, and this one puts me to sleep faster than all of them. Are you trying to drug your competition?"

"Don't be silly." He grinned. "You know I don't consider you competition."

She yanked the throw pillow from behind her and chucked it at his head.

Ryan sidestepped and caught it in mid-air. He dropped the lacy cushion by the couch arm and patted it. "Slow down and take a nap. A few hours won't make much difference, and it's not like you can canvas the streets with your swollen face. You look contagious."

"Everyone in town knows about my allergy."

"Everyone?" An ugly suspicion popped in his head, but he pushed it away. No one would slip Katherine a pineapple mickey on purpose. Working in the political world had taught him to keep his radar on, but he didn't need it in Sweetheart, Texas.

Katherine scraped her hand against the couch. "Ugh. The worst part is the itching."

"Will lotion help? I could buy it at the pharmacy."

"Actually, yes." Katherine grabbed a pad of paper and a pen from the coffee table and scribbled. "Ask Manny for this brand. Tell him it's for me. He knows about my allergy." She tore the top sheet off and passed it to him.

SHANNON SUE DUNLAP

"Got it." Ryan turned off his computer. He grabbed his wallet and walked to the door. "Is there anything else I can buy while I'm there?"

No response. He turned to find her staring into space.

"Katherine?"

Her eyes drifted shut, and her head plopped back on the couch.

Ryan kept his steps light as he exited. The store was close enough to walk, but the pharmacist was busy, and it took some searching to find the correct medication. He returned after thirty minutes, entered through the front door, and made sure it didn't bang shut.

Katherine was in the same spot he'd left her. She sat straight with her head tilted at a neck-cracking angle. Ryan tiptoed across the room, crouched next to the sofa, and nudged the hair away from her face. Bright red dots covered her forehead and nose, and her cheeks bulged around her lips. With the utmost care, he maneuvered her body to a horizontal position and propped the pillow she'd thrown at him under her head. She didn't stir.

"Katherine?" he whispered.

Ryan tapped her on the cheek, but her answer was a low moan. He lifted her legs to the cushions, then took the tube of medicated lotion from the plastic bag, unscrewed the top, and squeezed a generous amount on his finger.

He paused.

Should he call Deanna to do this? Putting medicine on someone's hives? Kind of personal.

Katherine gave another groan in her sleep and scratched her collarbone.

He rubbed the back of his neck. If he ever wrote an autobiography, no one would believe the Sweetheart chapter. Too outlandish.

Ryan stroked his lotion-covered finger over Katherine's cheeks and dabbed at the red dots until her face brought to mind a greasy snowstorm. He laughed under his breath. Any other woman would be mortified when she woke up, but Katherine Bruno would shrug it off.

Lifting her hand, he squeezed a small streak of salve on top. Ryan smoothed it over her skin with his thumb, rubbing in slow concentric circles. Glancing up, he found a pair of soft, half-open green eyes watching him.

Ryan stopped. "Are you awake? Don't misunderstand. I was —the medicine—it's supposed to help the itching—"

Her lids drifted shut.

One corner of Ryan's lips quirked. "So much for thinking it would be awkward."

He picked up her other hand and applied more lotion. She owed him big time for this.

SHE JUST MIGHT DIE.

Of what, she wasn't sure.

Pleasure? Embarrassment? Excitement?

All of the above.

Katherine did her best impression of Sleeping Beauty as Ryan gently worked the salve onto her itchy skin. His long fingers moved with gentle strength, making sure her entire hand was covered.

It was easily the most romantic moment of her life.

And she looked like a chipmunk with chickenpox.

Katherine wanted to scream with frustration. Why, God? Why couldn't there have been a less ugly reason for him to be holding her hand?

He finished and placed her fingers near her body. The rustle of his clothes told her he'd walked away. She dared to crack one eye a tiny bit. He halted at the trashcan by her desk and pulled out her smoothie cup. Ryan popped the plastic top off and stared inside. He remained motionless until curiosity overwhelmed her.

Opening both eyes, she tried to make her voice sound groggy. "What are you doing?"

He ignored her, swooped a finger in the cup, and scrutinized it.

Katherine pushed herself from the couch cushions and stood with a wobble. "I repeat, what are you doing?"

Oops. A little too awake, but too late now. If Ryan noticed, he didn't remark on her miraculous alertness.

He sniffed his hand and held it out in her direction. "Smells like pineapple pulp to me."

"What?" She jolted across the room and examined the evidence.

A few minuscule shreds of yellow covered his fingertips. He wiped them on the lip of the cup and set it on her desk.

Katherine touched her hot forehead. "I don't understand. I always order the same thing, and Susanna's too smart to get it wrong. I didn't even taste the pineapple."

"How much does it take to make you break out?"

"Not a lot. I once ate a spoonful on a dare in high school, and the nurse had to send me home."

"You said everyone in town knows about your allergy?"

She hesitated. "Yes. Why do you ask?"

He shoved a hand in his pocket, "It might not have been an accident. This reeks of sabotage."

"What!" She stared at the paper smoothie cup. "I don't—how could—that kind of stuff doesn't happen in Sweetheart."

"Do you have any enemies?"

"Of course not."

"How about people you've upset?"

A number of names scrolled through her brain. She'd never considered them enemies. More like people she'd annoyed. Since she'd lived in the same town for thirty years, it might be quicker to list the people who weren't upset with her. A little pineapple wouldn't kill her, only make her uncomfortable for a while. Was a disgruntled person trying to mess with her head?

"Do you really think someone spiked my smoothie on purpose?"

Ryan paused as if weighing his words. "Hard to say. But you shouldn't rule it out."

Katherine sorted through her feelings. Despair that anyone hated her so much. Anger at whoever the jerk was. And determination.

The last one grew until it overshadowed every other emotion. She would find the despicable pineapple pusher and make him quake in terror at her revenge. It had to be a customer where she'd bought the smoothie. Who did she remember seeing?

"Wait a minute. Susanna has a security camera inside the café. If someone slipped something in my drink, it might have caught it."

They both turned and headed for the door without another word. It was after she climbed into the passenger seat of Ryan's car when it hit her. He was helping her without being asked. They were working as a team.

Or even friends.

Their cold war must be over.

Now she had to find the faceless enemy who'd ambushed her with a smoothie sneak attack.

Chapter Thirteen

" **A** nd you never figured out who did it?" Deanna's outraged voice echoed from the office bathroom.

"No!" Katherine hollered. "Now stop primping and help me stuff these mailouts." She dumped a cardboard box on the coffee table and kneaded her spine.

Deanna wandered out, adjusting the cameo at the collar of her embroidered, white blouse. "How can you concentrate on work when a ruthless villain tried to poison you?"

"It was a minor allergic reaction."

"Are you sure you don't want to cancel and take a nap?" Her friend grabbed her by the arms and leaned close. "Your cheeks still look a little puffy."

"I'm fine." Katherine shook her off. "Ryan and I wasted three hours trying to track down the culprit. We checked the security footage at the café and interviewed the employees where I stopped at the grocery store. No one witnessed it."

"Awfully considerate of him to help you." Deanna lowered herself to a wingback chair and arranged her full skirt around her. "Did he seem," her eyes twinkled, "concerned for your welfare?"

"He was being a decent human." Her neck flushed, and she

turned, hoping Deanna would assume it was a leftover pineapple rash. She hadn't shared the details about the salve and Ryan applying it. No sense giving Deanna any more wrong ideas.

"You've upgraded him? That's better than what you called Ryan Park last week." Deanna raised herself up as she stared out the front window. "Well, lah-de-dah. Here comes the decent human now."

Katherine's heart raced. And she hated it. Just because she'd softened toward her arrogant office mate didn't mean she was ready to swoon at the sight of him.

Ryan swung the front door open. He stepped to the side and flourished his arm to the inside of the office. "Please come in, ladies. I wish you were visiting me, but I suspect you're heading for the enemy's camp."

Lanette Johnson entered in a velvet aquamarine tracksuit with pearl accents on the pant seams. "You suspect right. And I'm the general, so be on your best behavior."

"Yes, ma'am." He saluted with two fingers. "I'll be over at my desk spying on your plans and preparing my counterattack."

"Oh, you."

Lanette swatted his arm and readjusted the straps of her giant pink purse. Her sidekick Elise followed and mirrored her gesture, giving the handsome man's arm a gentle love tap. He grabbed his bicep and made a dramatic grimace.

"No time for social niceties." Katherine beckoned them. "We've got work to do."

Ryan gave an exaggerated head waggle as he retreated to his side of the office. Lanette and Elise set their overstuffed purses on a side table and joined the girls at the couch.

Katherine motioned to the box on the coffee table. "I've got the supplies." She withdrew a bunch of envelopes. "Okay, troops. Let's stuff these while we plan the schedule for the Bullhorn Beauty Pageant this weekend."

Deanna groaned and slumped in her chair.

Elise collapsed on the couch. "Whose brilliant idea was it to combine campaign meetings with pageant prep? Between the two, I don't get home until all hours of the night. It's exhausting planning multiple big events."

"The election has never been a big event 'til now." Lanette settled in one of the brocade chairs and pulled her phone from her pocket. "No one bothered to run against my husband for the last decade. He always won by default. This year he has to work for the win."

"What do you mean the win?" Elise jumped up. "Do you think we'll lose?"

"I didn't mean that. Calm down."

She sank to the cushions, her mouth pinched in an unhappy pucker. "Still, it sounds kind of—"

"Give me a minute." Lanette waved an impatient hand as she texted. "I have to answer the decorator's question. I wish Susanna Sheppard hadn't taken the year off from the pageant committee. She always handled these pesky details."

"She's busy being a newlywed." Elise giggled.

"I'll say." Deanna nudged Elise with the toe of her saddle shoe. "With a one-month engagement before they tied the knot, I imagine those two were in a hurry."

"Here are the receipts for the envelopes." Katherine passed them to Elise as she sat. "Be sure you keep a record of how much the campaign spends." She pushed the stacks of paper on the table closer. "If we start right away, we can knock this out in an hour and then discuss the pageant arrangements."

"Tack a few minutes on the schedule for the Candy Hearts Festival." Lanette looked up from her phone. "Valentine's Day will be here before we know it."

Her constituents moaned, but she ignored them. "It's Sweetheart's biggest moneymaker. Can't disappoint the tourists, or they won't come back next time."

Elise scooted her chair to the table. "How about you, Katie? Are you baking something for the cake auction this year?"

Katherine cringed. "I'm a terrible cook. Why put myself and the poor guy who might buy it through the trouble?"

"Now, dear." Elise nudged her. "It's not about the food. It's the company that comes with it."

"Another strike against me."

A suspicious choking sounded from Ryan's side of the office. Katherine shot a glare his direction. He was turned away, his shoulders vibrating.

"Don't be so hard on yourself, honey." Lanette picked a piece of lint from the sleeve of her velvet tracksuit. "You're a strong-minded woman. It'll take a man with gumption to match you. I'm sure there's someone around here who appreciates your finer qualities." She jerked her head at Ryan's desk and wiggled her brows.

"Mr. Park," Elise twittered, "do you have a sweet tooth? You should come to our annual cake auction in February. It's the highlight of the Candy Hearts Festival."

Ryan swung his chair around, his trademark grin gracing his lips. "I'd love to, ladies. But I don't plan to be here much longer. Once the mayoral race is over, I'll return to New York."

A chorus of disappointed protests met his declaration.

Katherine kept her attention on the mailouts. Why were they so shocked? She knew Ryan wouldn't stay forever, but it hadn't hit her how close his eventual departure was. He'd fly back to his big-city lifestyle and forget all about Sweetheart.

And her.

She grabbed an envelope. No time for sentimental garbage. She had an election campaign to plan and a beauty pageant for cows to attend on the weekend. Her life was full enough without adding a potential heartbreak to the mix.

Two hours flew by as the women chatted and readied the flyers. It might have been finished in half the time if there weren't so much talking. The noise level decreased the moment Elise and Lanette exited.

Deanna gave Katherine a hug at the door. "See you later, sugar."

After her friend left, Katherine locked the deadbolt and leaned against the jamb with a sigh of relief.

"Sorry about the racket." She looked Ryan's way, but he remained silent. His head bent over his laptop, fingers tapping the keys. "Did we bother you?"

He still didn't answer.

Katherine wandered over. As she drew near, she noted a small white bud in his ear. She plucked the device out, and he jumped. The muted sounds of symphony music drifted from the tiny piece of plastic.

"Are they gone?" He checked the couch.

"Cheater." Katherine waved the bud under his nose. "I had to listen to two hours of gossip while you enjoyed the New York Philharmonic."

He relaxed in his seat and propped his hands behind his head. "I bet I got a lot more done too."

"On the contrary." She threw the earbud against his chest, and he caught it. "We were noisy, but productive."

A ringing interrupted.

Ryan lifted his phone and checked the caller ID. "I've got to take this. It's my sister."

Katherine turned away to give him a modicum of privacy in the small office. She'd heard him talk with his sister, Victoria Park, several times in the past month. Their close relationship radiated through the cheerful banter, and he always ended their conversations with a smile on his face.

"Hey, Vic." Ryan sat in his desk chair and stretched his legs out. "What's up?"

Katherine returned to the coffee table, gathered a stack of envelopes, and placed them in the box. Ryan talked for a few minutes when his tone changed mid-sentence.

"No. Don't put Dad on the phone. I don't ... Vic. Don't—" His shoulders straightened, and he sat up tall. "Hello, Dad."

Katherine pretended to work as she cast covert glances his way. Ryan didn't say much. He stood and paced in front of his desk.

"Yes, sir." He rubbed the nape of his neck. "Is it? Guess I forgot. I imagine there's a church somewhere in town."

"We have several!" Katherine shouted across the room.

Ryan glared at her and turned his back. "Yes, sir." He moved a pencil to a different section in his organizer. "Yes. I'll try. Goodbye." He tossed the phone on his desk. "Thanks for your help. Now I have to go to church on Sunday instead of enjoying some much-needed sleep."

"What a great idea." She gave him a tiny round of applause. "Sounds like your father is much closer to God than you."

"He'd better be. He's a minister."

"You're a preacher's kid?" Katherine dropped the pile of papers she was holding.

"Surprised?"

"Yes. No! I mean," she shrugged, "I pictured you growing up in a liberal arts professor's home across from Central Park."

Ryan snorted. "My sister and I were raised on a pew in Queens. I assure you I was quite the well-behaved lad. I sang in the choir. Went on mission trips. Believe it or not, I even attended seminary for a semester. If you totaled the hours I've spent in church, they'd easily top any campaign I've ever worked on." He moaned and threaded his fingers through his hair. "And I'll add a few more this Sunday."

"It'll do you good." Katherine smirked. "And think how happy it will make your father. Are you two close?"

His small laugh sounded forced. "My father tends to be quiet and reserved. It runs in his family. They've bred the stoic macho type for centuries."

"Is your mom's side reserved, as well?"

"Not the slightest bit. They're passionate Italians who still cook their own secret spaghetti sauce. Mom's extrovert nature more than made up for Dad's lack of communication."

It struck her how little she truly knew about Ryan Park. Now that she'd gotten past her prejudices, she wanted to hear more.

Katherine perched on the edge of a chair and leaned forward. "Was it a case of opposites attract?"

"To say the least." Ryan powered down his computer and closed the lid. "They met at seminary, married, and planned to live in South Korea as missionaries, but mom got pregnant with me. Instead, they took a multi-cultural church in Queens."

"A mission field in their own backyard. Nice. Are they still there?"

"Dad is." He turned away and slipped his laptop into the padded, black bag. "Mom passed away eight years ago."

Katherine swallowed—a difficult task when she'd just placed her foot in her mouth. Again.

"I—I'm sorry."

"Me too." He straightened his stapler to a perfect ninety-degree angle and stood. "What about your parents?"

Katherine placed the last stack of newly-stuffed envelopes in the box. "They died in a car accident when I was twelve. Drunk driver."

Ryan cleared his throat. "My turn to be sorry."

"No need." She lifted the box and carried it to the only clear corner on her side of the room. "It was a long time ago."

It didn't hurt to talk about her parents' death. What hurt were all the long, lonely years that followed.

"My parents were opposites, too, but they made marriage look fun. Dad had this special tune he whistled as he came home from work. When Mom heard him, she raced for the door and gave him a big kiss."

"Did you live in a Fifties sitcom?"

"I know, right?" She chuckled. "But they really were crazy about each other. When mom lost her temper, which she did often—"

"You must take after her."

"Shh." Katherine held a finger to her lips. "My dad would

wrap her in a bear hug and wiggle around the room until she was laughing too hard to be mad anymore. I always wanted that to be me and my husband someday."

Silence stretched. The ticking from the old grandfather clock on the wall boomed like a cannon in the stillness.

Ryan swept her with a gaze. "But?"

"But I never found the man brave enough to take me on. And my temper too."

He picked up his computer bag. "You are a force to be reckoned with."

She gave one short jerk of her chin, unsure if he was insulting her or stating a fact. "Well—"

"I admire that about you." A genuine grin of camaraderie lifted his lips as he walked to the door. "Goodnight, Katherine."

His words knocked the breath from her body, and it took a moment to recover from the impact. She called after him as he left.

"See you in church."

Chapter Fourteen

The cream of Sweetheart society milled around the large town square as hints of purple and dusky rose faded from the expansive sky. Strings of old-fashioned bulbs swayed from the lampposts, casting a warm glow on the festivities. Citizens wore homemade T-shirts declaring which cow they supported in the annual Bullhorn Beauty Pageant, and refreshment booths offered a fragrant assortment of pies, cookies, homemade fudge, and other sweet delights.

Katherine sucked in a whiff of cake-scented air. Home sugary home. Should she sample Susanna's red velvet or start with Mrs. Day's chocolate chip caramel brownies?

"Step right up. Step right up." Willy Walker's carnival barker delivery shattered the peaceful ambiance of the summer evening. "Come and meet the finest mayor in Texas."

She rolled her eyes at the unwelcome interruption. Ryan's team had organized their flashy booth in the most visible spot on the square. He called the locals by name and shook their hands as they passed. LED lights scrolled the slogan *Harry has heart* in all its multi-colored glory, while his volunteers passed out flyers with QR codes.

"Click on the little black box." Mayor Johnson hooked his

thumbs in the armpits of his suede vest. "You'll hear a special message about the great things coming to Sweetheart."

Katherine studied the high-tech opposition. Was she doing enough to promote her own candidate?

Lanette *tsk-tsked* from behind their much smaller campaign table. "That man loves anything electronic."

"It's not a bad strategy." Katherine faced her boss. "People use their phones for everything. We should have made codes."

"Codes schmodes." Elise waved a platter of goodies from her spot by the curb. "Nothing can compete with my banana bread."

Lanette pulled her bedazzled western jacket from a metal folding chair. She slipped it over her rosy silk blouse, took a compact mirror from her purse, and fluffed her blonde hair. "Prepare to be amazed, girls. I'm about to unleash our secret weapon."

"What?" Katherine moved closer. "You didn't tell me about any—"

"Stop worrying, honey." Lanette patted her cheek. "All will be revealed soon."

Katherine bit her lower lip. What new embarrassment awaited? No matter how hard she tried, their campaign was always giving Ryan Park a new reason to flash his snarky smile. She searched the crowd until she found him. He mingled with the locals, unaware of the "secret weapon" her candidate had in store.

Lanette shoved the compact in her pocket and waved at someone behind Katherine. "Here they come."

High-pitched voices rippled. She turned and beheld the entire Ladies Auxiliary headed their way in matching fluorescent T-shirts with pink rhinestones spelling *Bet on Lanette*.

Mary Thibodeaux led the charge, wheeling an antiquated karaoke machine. She propped the lopsided device against a fire hydrant. "Sorry we're late. I wanted to practice one last time before we performed. Warm up your voices, girls."

The auxiliary members fanned out in a wide half-circle. Some rolled their lips, and others hummed the scale. The dread in Katherine's gut spread to her fingertips. Her pastor's wife sang at least one solo every Sunday, but what kind of song would be appropriate in this setting?

Mrs. Thibodeaux checked the battery in her cordless microphone, slipped a cassette tape in the slot, and nodded. "Ready."

Lanette pointed a finger. "Let 'em have it, Mary."

She hit play, and a gospel organ blared.

Katherine recognized the melody of *When the Saints Go Marching In*. Was the minister's wife going to hold a revival meeting on the street?

Mrs. Thibodeaux ooohed and wailed. She conducted her hand like she was directing the church choir and sang.

"Oh, when Lanette
Shows up and wins
Oh, when Lanette
Shows up and wins
Oh Lord, I know
You'll give her that number
When Sweetheart votes
And Laaaa-neeeeeeeeette wiiiiiiins."

The Ladies Auxiliary swayed behind her, not always in the same direction. They bumped and jived as the music wound up for another chorus.

Mary shoved a fist in the air. *"Oh, when Lanette."*

They echoed her the second time through. *"Oh, when Lanette."*

One by one, an audience gathered. They clapped and bobbed their heads, and a few brave souls sang along. Others recorded with their phones.

Elise ditched her banana bread, fetched a tambourine from under the table, and smacked it against her palm—completely undeterred by her lack of rhythm.

Katherine covered her face. She didn't dare look across the square at Ryan. Could her campaign be any less professional?

But the crowd loved it. That was the important part. Right?

Katherine peeked through her fingers. People cheered as Mary Thibodeaux hit the final note with a glorious crescendo, and her listeners hollered for more.

Mrs. Thibodeaux beamed. "An encore? If you insist." Awkward silence followed while she rewound her cassette tape. "Pass the offering basket while I get the music ready!"

Elise grabbed the contributions box at the end of their table and wove through the onlookers. A few waved it away, but others slipped bills into the slot. Katherine caught sight of Ryan's dumbstruck expression from the opposite side of the street. She met his gaze and gave him a two-fingered salute. He still had a lot to learn about what worked in Sweetheart, Texas.

RYAN LEANED against his deserted display table and listened to the Ladies Auxiliary sing a third rendition of what might euphemistically be called Lanette Johnson's campaign song. A shrieking microphone from the stage at the end of the square interrupted their final chorus.

"Ladies and gentlemen." Deanna Day walked centerstage in a blue-and-white checkered gingham dress with her golden hair in a milkmaid style—braided and looped over her ears. "Please come and take your seats. It's time to begin our annual Bullhorn Beauty Pageant."

The spectators wandered away and set up their camping chairs around the main event.

Ryan wound through the small crowd to Katherine and waited while she told Elise where to store the campaign contributions before he approached. "Your team put on quite the show."

She raised her chin. "The personal touch will beat out fancy lighting any day of the week."

He bowed his head in gracious acknowledgment. "Are you going to watch the pageant?"

"I wouldn't miss it. You have no idea what you're about to experience."

Ryan motioned for her to lead the way. They walked together to the edge of the crowd and found an empty park bench at the back. As they took a seat, Deanna finished introducing the first bovine contestant.

A docile brown and white Hereford ambled up the ramp on the side of the stage. It wore a curly white wig a la George Washington, and a star-spangled ruffle hung around its neck. The owner stood with a saxophone next to its wrinkled muzzle and played an ear-splitting version of the national anthem.

First a gospel choir campaign song and now this? Ryan pressed his twitching lips together as the rancher finished his squeaky solo. The crowd whistled and cheered for the melodious entry.

"That was very," Ryan cleared his throat, "patriotic."

"It can't compare to Broadway, but wait." She crossed her arms. "You'll love the celebrity look-a-like portion of the competition."

He shut his eyes and moaned. "I'm not sure I can keep a straight face."

"Why bother? None of us do." She laughed. "The whole point of this pageant was to lift the citizens' spirits. It started in the Forties during World War II, when so many sons and fathers were overseas. I imagine they'd be proud to hear it's still bringing people joy."

"What I don't understand is why there aren't more visitors." Ryan studied the modest crowd. He recognized almost everyone in the audience. "I'd expect the tourists to devour this kind of kitschy extravaganza."

"A few folks drive in from the surrounding towns, but it's not well-known outside of Sweetheart."

"Why not? You publicize your big Valentine's Day celebration, don't you?"

"The Candy Hearts Festival? Absolutely. It's the biggest event of the year. The profits bring enough revenue for the local businesses to pay the bills."

Ryan scratched his head. "If you let the same audience know about a beauty pageant involving cosplaying cows, the businesses could make enough to cover the bills and have some left over. It's such an easy drive from multiple big cities. The perfect day trip for lovers of the absurd. I imagine ..."

His voice petered away as he took in her expression. Her parted lips. Her stiff body. Had he offended her again?

"What? Did I—"

"Brilliant," Katherine whispered. "Why hasn't anyone thought of it before?" She stood up, turning in all directions as her voice rose. "We could build a whole new festival around the pageant. Local artists could design cow-themed products!"

Annoyed faces pointed their way. The current bull on stage in a full-length astronaut suit shook its head and mooed.

"Shh." Ryan tugged on her sleeve, and she flopped onto the bench. "I'm glad you appreciate the idea, but you're spooking the livestock."

She grabbed his arm with both hands and leaned toward him. "It would pack the Sweetheart Inn and Mrs. Showalter's bed-and-breakfast too. She was telling me last week how bad business has been. This could be a lifesaver for her. Why didn't we advertise the pageant?"

Ryan enjoyed the fireworks in her emerald eyes. For a change, it wasn't frustration at him setting them off. "Don't worry too much. I'm willing to bet this inventive town has something else besides a Candy Hearts Festival and a Bullhorn Beauty Pageant. Are there any other local celebrations tourists might find appealing?"

"I don't know." Katherine's fingers tapped his skin as she thought.

Each touch sent tiny shockwaves through his bicep. Her fingers loosened but remained on his arm. Did Katherine realize she was clinging to him?

"Do you think people would enjoy a Shakespeare-themed cookoff? Willy Walker dreamed it up a few years ago—Puck Pancakes, Et tu Brute Barbecue, Hamlet Hamhocks."

Ryan chuckled. "You've got another winner. Especially if you invited visitors to participate with their own dishes. Make it a weekend-long contest with a trophy at the finish."

Katherine released him. Despite the warm summer evening, Ryan's skin felt cold where her fingers had been. She didn't say a word for the rest of the pageant. He imagined the gears turning in her head. Katherine made notes on her phone and mumbled softly to herself with a quiet laugh here and there.

Deanna Day announced the grand prize winner as she placed a tiara on the head of the George Washington cow. After a standing ovation, she dismissed the crowd, but Katherine continued working. The hum of crickets replaced conversations as people grabbed their lawn chairs and left. Ryan waited in silence so as not to disrupt her brainstorming. When she finished, only a few stragglers remained.

"Is it over?" She scanned the town square.

"Mm-hmm." Ryan stood and stretched his arms over his head. "You appeared to be in the zone, and I didn't want to interrupt you. Get any good ideas?"

"A million." She hopped up. "And it's thanks to you."

He basked in the unfamiliar glow of her praise. "It was no big deal."

"You may have saved several small businesses with your suggestion. It's a very big deal." She threw her arms around his neck and squeezed. "The entire town of Sweetheart thanks you."

He didn't know about the whole town. All he could concentrate on was the soft woman pressed against him. His arms automatically raised. This was his rival. He should push her away. Instead, his hands hovered over her back before settling on her waist. Why not enjoy the brief moment of harmony?

"I'm happy to see you youngsters getting along." Mayor Johnson ambled up, his wife at his side.

Katherine jerked away and tugged at the edge of her T-shirt.

Lanette nodded and threaded her arm through her husband's. "You're so right, precious. We need to keep this competition friendly."

Katherine cleared her throat. "I was just thanking Ryan, I mean Mr. Park, for the great idea he shared. It would create a whole new stream of revenue for the town, Mayor Johnson. Can I discuss it with you?"

She looked at Ryan, and the warmth of her smile knocked him sideways. Confusion followed. Since when did her approval mean so much to him?

"Sounds great." Mayor Johnson nodded. "Once we get the election finished and construction begins on the town hall, I want you to tell me all about it."

Lanette withdrew her arm from his. "Didn't you hear what she said? This can't wait. It could mean cash coming into Sweetheart, unlike your town hall plan."

Ryan winced. His gaze cut to Katherine. A similar expression appeared on her face, and she rubbed a finger between her brows. So much for keeping it friendly.

Mayor Johnson smoothed his hair as he cast a nervous peek around the group. "Can we discuss this later, Lanette? You haven't even heard what Katherine's proposal is. Why get fired up?"

Lanette spread her feet apart and squared her shoulders. "Anything has to be better than the economic black hole you and your cronies created."

"Black hole? I'm moving Sweetheart into the twenty-first century, but all you can do is nag."

"You're so deep in the wrong you've lost all perspective."

Lanette poked a finger at his chest. "I'm afraid it will take a major wake-up call for you to listen to reason."

"Don't patronize me." Mayor Johnson stomped his foot. "I know what I'm doing."

Ryan turned his body to give them a semblance of privacy. It was a useless courtesy. The two yelled loud enough to be heard from one end of Main Street to the other.

"I'll bring you to your senses if it's the last thing I do," Lanette bellowed. "I challenge you to a debate!"

"Here?" Her husband's voice wavered.

"No, precious. Somewhere public where the whole town can attend. Let's lay out exactly what our platforms are and what each of us wants to do with Sweetheart."

Ryan's gaze met Katherine's. The metaphorical gap between them widened—two unwilling observers in this perverse battle of the spouses. She broke eye contact first and dug in her purse.

If she wasn't going to raise an objection, it was his responsibility.

"Mayor Johnson, I planned to arrange a debate for you both, but it takes a while to pick the venue, set a time, alert the media."

"Tomorrow night." Lanette slapped her thigh.

Ryan started to object, but his boss beat him to it.

"Won't work." Mayor Johnson held up a hand. "It's Sunday, and we both have a church board meeting."

Ryan exhaled. At least his candidate had some sense.

"How about Monday?" the mayor said. "No, wait. We scheduled dinner with the Walkers. Tuesday, then?"

Ryan ground his teeth. Both sides lacked a grasp of the obvious. A proper debate took time to prepare. Why was Katherine typing in her phone instead of objecting? Was he the only one who saw how ludicrous the situation was?

"Tuesday?" He stepped between the couple. "Mrs. Johnson, I realize this is a small town and you have a lot of contacts, but there are certain protocols to follow. Arranging a debate in three days is impossible."

Lanette stared over his shoulder. "Is it impossible, Katie?"

Katherine joined them and waved her cell. "I texted the high school principal. She said the auditorium is booked for play practice but offered the gym as an alternative."

Mayor Johnson rubbed his ear. "I'm not sure this is a good idea, Lanette. I don't fancy hanging out our dirty laundry for the whole town to see."

She raised her pointed nose. "Whatever do you mean? I assure you I will be perfectly civil during our debate. If anyone makes this personal, it won't be me. Now let's go home, I've got a speech to write."

Lanette spun on her heel and stalked off, leaving Mayor Johnson to scamper after her, complaining all the way.

Ryan rounded on Katherine. "You must realize this is a terrible idea. Neither candidate is prepared for a debate."

He half-expected her to blow up at him, but she smiled instead.

"I'll give you a pass since you gifted me with that wonderful idea earlier." Katherine patted his arm. "Allow me to return the favor by giving you a piece of advice." She stood on tiptoe and whispered in his ear. "Don't underestimate me or my candidate."

His stomach dipped, whether from the challenge or her proximity, he couldn't tell. But one thing was certain, he felt like a soldier on the battlefield who'd forgotten his armor at home.

Chapter Fifteen

A morning stroll through the neighborhood had sounded so relaxing in Katherine's head. The perfect way to unwind after the pageant chaos. Take the dogs for a walk. Go home and shower, with plenty of time left over to dress for church. But she hadn't counted on the constant battle with the hyperactive puppy on her right.

"Bella, stop it."

She tried to steer the terrier away from a discarded paper bag. The leash pulled taut between them. Mild-tempered Romeo stayed nearby without a care for his sister's antics. Katherine made a mental battle plan as she walked the dogs. Church was the perfect place to spread the word about Tuesday night's debate.

"No, Bella!" She blocked a tempting puddle from the puppy.

A movement ahead drew Katherine's attention. She studied Renae Smith spearing trash along the side of the road with a pointed stick. The blonde's ample curves were hidden under an orange reflective safety vest.

Katherine and Renae weren't exactly what you'd call close, but a vote was a vote. She worked up a polite expression and approached. "Good morning, Renae."

"Maybe it's good for you." She didn't even look up. "You don't have to collect garbage."

"Because I don't do stupid things like setting flower boxes on fire."

Oops. Not a good way to influence people. Pointing out their past criminal activity.

Renae stabbed a piece of paper with the stick. "I played a few practical jokes. Nothing that warranted a thousand hours of community service. Lanette was the one who suggested this park cleanup on my day off. Remind me to thank her." She poked at a pile of cartons. "It's humiliating. Do you have any idea how it feels to be a social pariah?"

"More than you realize."

The puppies jerked their leashes in two opposite directions.

"Sure. People joke about your temper, but that's nothing." Renae tugged at the safety vest. "This orange might as well be scarlet like the book they made us read in high school. The one about the woman with the *A* on her chest. The folks in Sweetheart will never forgive my mistakes."

"Yes, they will." Katherine bent to grab a foam cup from the grass. "These people are soft as cotton balls on the inside. Give them time, and they'll let it go."

"But they'll never let me live it down."

Katherine shrugged. "Small-town folks have long memories. I speak from my own experience with public humiliation."

Renae snickered. "Remember the time you dumped a pail of water over Billy Walker's head when he asked you to the prom."

Katherine snatched a crumpled water bottle from under a bush and tossed the trash in the bag. "He wasn't really asking. I knew he'd made a bet with his friends I'd say yes."

"A date's a date." Renae sighed. "It's been so long since my last one, there's an inch of dust on my dressy stilettos."

Katherine didn't own a pair of stilettos, but the dust would be deeper than an inch if she did. Her last date had been at the community college with a guy who'd just moved to town. He hadn't been around long enough to learn of her volatile reputation.

"Lah-dee-dah." Renae's wide eyes pointed behind Katherine. "Finally, something good happens."

Bella yipped and strained at her leash. Katherine turned and saw Ryan jogging around the corner in gray sweats.

"Ah, my sworn political enemy."

Her sarcasm was more from habit than actual antagonism. In fact, she was feeling downright courteous to her next-door neighbor. She tried not to note the wide stretch of his shoulders or the sweat dripping from the curve of his square jaw.

He spotted them, waved, and headed their way. Renae plunged her trash-collecting stick in the grass and whipped a compact from her jeans pocket. She powdered her nose, wiped at the corners of her lips, and pushed the stray hairs from her forehead in five seconds flat. Putting the makeup away, she showed both rows of teeth like she was walking a beauty pageant runway.

"Good morning, ladies." Ryan approached and bent to rub an ecstatic Bella on the head.

The Velcro tabs crackled as Renae whipped the safety vest off and tossed it in the trash bag. "So good to see you again, Ryan." She extended a hand with long red fingernails, palm down. "*Bonjour.* You are the brightest spot in my day. *Oui. Oui.*"

Katherine shuddered at the fake French accent. But Ryan's response brought a whole new level of phony to the conversation.

He took the proffered hand, and his mouth widened in that open, welcoming beam he reserved for campaign outings. His real smile was more of a smirk. No teeth showing, with one corner quirked up.

"Southern manners with a dash of Paris. *Tres Magnifique.*" He gave a courtly bow, and Renae giggled.

She jabbed her elbow in Katie's arm and said in a fake

whisper, "He's the cutest thing this town has seen in a long time. And you called him the enemy."

Ryan glanced at Katherine. Her cheeks heated, though she'd have called him that to his face.

"Don't blame her too much." He pushed a thick strand of silky, black hair off his forehead. "It's true we're on opposite sides of the political aisle. Tell me, Renae, have you decided who you're voting for in the mayoral race?"

One thinly-plucked eyebrow raised, and her bright red lips turned upward. "I can't say for sure, but I imagine I could be convinced if the right person were to ask."

Katherine suppressed the childish urge to pretend she was throwing up. Did the woman have to be so obvious? If Sweetheart held an election for Town Flirt, Renae would win in a landslide.

Katherine lacked the patience flirting required. If you liked someone, tell them. If you didn't, same thing. It saved a lot of heartache and confusion. Not that her philosophy brought her any success. Even the few men who returned her interest were eventually driven away by her strong, independent personality.

Ryan didn't appear turned off by Renae. On the contrary, he was grinning. He pulled a card from his pocket along with a pen and wrote on the back.

Who carried business cards in their sweatpants? Katherine snorted before she could stop herself.

Ryan's gaze raised to hers for a brief second, but he kept writing.

"Here you are." He held the paper out to Renae. "This is my office phone number in case you'd ever consider helping Mayor Johnson's campaign."

"Oh, I'm an excellent helper."

"I can tell." Ryan motioned to the half-full bag. "Not many people spend their weekends picking up trash. You must love your community."

Renae had the decency to blush as she pushed the hair

behind both ears. "Oh, it's nothing. Do you train your volunteers personally?" She leaned close enough for him to count the false eyelashes on her turquoise-shadowed lids.

He laughed and took a sizable step back. "We're not a one-horse operation. I have a whole team. Please call if you decide to join us."

Katherine took pity on him and interrupted. "Sorry, Renee. We have to get a move on. Ryan and I have someplace to be."

A leash wrapped around her legs and jerked her off-balance. She stumbled, and Ryan caught her with one arm.

"We do?" Confusion and relief warred in Ryan's expression. "Oh, right. We do."

"Headed somewhere special, Katie?" Renae's pageant smile didn't quite reach her eyes.

"The most special." Katherine nodded. "We're going to church."

"To church?" Ryan's head reared.

"You told your Dad you'd check out one of our local congregations. I'm helping you keep that promise." She passed the leashes to Ryan. "Would you give the puppies water while I change? I'll meet you at my car in fifteen minutes."

"Katherine." His tone warned her he wanted to argue, but Renee moved to his side, and he hesitated. "Fifteen minutes."

Katherine kept an innocent expression as she turned away. This probably wasn't what Jesus meant when He said to be fishers of men, but she'd reeled in a big one this time.

RYAN SHIFTED in his seat and straightened the cuffs of his dark blue dress shirt. It had been eight years since he'd set foot in a church. How could they still be singing the same songs? The old familiar hymn ignited memories from his childhood. Sleeping underneath a pew while his father preached. Running through the Sunday school halls with friends. Getting in trouble later.

He laughed to himself. His poor dad had spent many a Sunday night lecturing his son on what he'd done wrong Sunday morning. His mother was the buffer—always finding a way to smooth things over between them. It was her grace-filled version of love that led Ryan to his own faith. He'd considered following in his father's footsteps and joining the ministry—until life forced him to accept reality.

What was the point of serving a God who either didn't exist or wasn't listening? Either way, it was a mistake he didn't plan to repeat.

Still, this didn't have to be a total waste of time. He observed the faces around him. Harry and Lanette Johnson sat in the front pew with Willy and Elise Walker beside them. A few rows behind, Jud Watson picked at his beard. Two seats to the right, he noted a family of five he hadn't met yet.

This was a prime opportunity to connect with the outlying citizens of Sweetheart. Let the service soften them up first, then swoop in and introduce himself.

Katherine should have considered the drawbacks when she'd invited him. It was asking a wolf to dine with the sheep. He smirked and glanced beside him. His lips drooped. Katherine's tiny nose was pink at the tip, and her eyes welled with tears. Had she read his thoughts?

He whispered from the side of his mouth. "Are you okay?"

"It's this song." She sniffled. "It always gets me."

He sighed. Who could predict the actions of this explosive woman? Shouting at the top of her lungs one minute. Soft and weepy the next. The usher passed by and did a swift U-turn. The burly gentleman in the three-piece suit with the carefully combed handlebar mustache studied Katherine and eyed him with suspicion. Ryan straightened and slid away an inch. Did the old man think he was the cause of her crying?

Ryan averted his eyes and scratched the side of his neck. He pretended to listen intently as Pastor Thibodeaux walked to the pulpit and read his text. Hopefully, the minister wasn't long-winded.

He ran through his mental to-do list. Now that his volunteers were lined up, it was time to train them to be influencers—posting on social media before the debate and spreading positive word-of-mouth stories about Mayor Johnson. He managed to plan out the whole week by the time the organist hit the first chord for the closing song. The entire congregation stood, opened their hymnals, and sang with gusto.

As soon as the last note ended, Lanette made a beeline his way. She slipped into the pew in front of him and braced her hands on the back rim. "Glad to see you in church, young man."

Ryan nodded. "Good morning, Lanette."

Elise Walker pushed through the sea of bodies filing down the middle aisle. She squeezed into their pew and plopped beside Ryan.

"Hello, you two. You looked so cute sitting together during service."

How had she noticed from several rows in front of them?

Katherine scooted a little to the side. "Lanette, was there something you needed?"

"Hmmm?" Her eyebrows raised. "Oh, yes. Katie, will you research some numbers for me? I'd do it myself, but there's a church board meeting. We need a game plan for the debate. How about we focus—"

"Save the details for later." Katherine jumped up. "When it's less crowded." She jerked her head in his direction.

Ryan pointed at his chest. "What's the matter? Afraid I'll steal your talking points?"

Elise elbowed him. "You know what they say, a closed mouth won't catch any flies. Don't feel bad. Katie's that way with everybody. She wouldn't let me tell my husband about our pageant booth for fear he'd pass information along to Harry." She patted his arm. "Have you got any plans for lunch? You're welcome to eat at my house."

Ryan rose from his seat. "I might take you up on the offer. My fridge is overflowing with takeout containers."

"Good." Elise maneuvered her wide hips as she stood between the pews and looped her purse strap over her arm. "What about you, Katie?"

A thunderous throat-clearing sounded to their right. They turned in unison and found Sheriff Garcia standing at the end of the pew near the wall, clasping a tan Stetson.

"Pardon me for the interruption, ladies."

Ryan noted he wasn't included in the apology. He muffled a chuckle. Even the law knew who ran this town.

"Sheriff," Lanette approached him and thumped a hand against his chest, "I've been trying to get you to church for years. What brought about this miracle?"

He kneaded the hat brim with restless fingers. "I'm afraid this isn't a social call. We've received a tip I have to check out. It must be a mistake, but"—he straightened his spine—"but it's my duty to follow every lead."

"Spit it out, Sheriff," Katherine said. "What's the problem?"

He twisted the Stetson around and around. "A person has accused Mrs. Walker of campaign fraud."

Even though the sheriff had spoken in a low tone, conversations halted from the altar to the exit. Every jaw in the room dropped, except for Elise Walker's. Her lips closed. She froze without so much as a blink.

Lanette pounded a fist on the pew. "That's ridiculous! How can you suggest such a thing?"

"I know it's crazy." The sheriff jammed his hat on his head. "But someone claims they saw Mrs. Walker spending campaign funds for her own personal use."

"Who?" Katherine propped her hands on her hips.

"There's the rub." He surveyed the sanctuary and tugged the hat back off his head. "We don't exactly know. It was an anonymous tip shoved under the door before we arrived at the station this morning."

Katherine snorted. "I've witnessed Elise labor over her little brown notebook for weeks. Last Thursday, she wouldn't let Lanette spend three dollars on hairspray, afraid it wouldn't be a legitimate expense."

"Wonderful." The sheriff nodded. "If you can show me your logbook and the receipts for any purchases made, it should be sufficient evidence this is all a misunderstanding."

Elise whimpered.

"Don't be scared, honey." Lanette scooted around the sheriff and shoved past Katherine to stand by Elise. She rubbed her friend's back. "Just show him your book, and this will be over."

"I"—she gulped—"I lost the receipts."

"You what?" Katherine's voice rose.

The older woman's eyes filled. "I'm not sure what happened. I kept such careful track of all our purchases, but when I got home last night and checked my purse, the receipts were gone." She flopped onto the pew, buried her face in her hands, and broke into noisy sobs.

Sheriff Garcia groaned. "I'm afraid this complicates things."

Katherine's posture stiffened. "If you think I'm going to let you take an innocent—"

Ryan cringed. What was about to fly out of her mouth? He pushed past her and blocked her from the sheriff's view. "Excuse me, sir. As the manager for the opposition, I've had plenty of opportunities to observe this team. There's no way Mrs. Walker stole anything." He widened his stance to keep Katherine from barging around him. Getting herself locked up wouldn't help Elise or anyone else.

"I'm well aware of her good character." The sheriff ruffled his thick, curly gray hair. "If she could come to the station—"

"You're arresting me?" Elise's wail carried across the room.

A flock of women descended on them from every corner of the church. They crowded around the huddled Elise, smoothing her hair and cooing.

"Why, darling." Mary Thibodeaux fluttered over. "What's the matter?"

Lanette stood in front of her friend with arms crossed. "You'll arrest her over my dead body."

Sheriff Garcia surveyed the onslaught of women. "I didn't—"

The noise level rose in tandem. A chorus of female voices added their promised corpses to the fray.

"Please." Garcia raised one finger. "Mrs. Johnson, I—If you'll allow me to—Ladies, there's no need for—Shut up!"

A shocked silence ensued. For three seconds. Followed by outraged protestations and offended head-shaking.

"I'm not arresting her." Sheriff Garcia's soothing tone did little to hush the pandemonium. "I want to ask her a few questions at the office. She can go home as soon as we're done."

"Then why not do it here?" Katherine jostled Ryan from behind. "Elise will be much more at ease if she's not sitting in a place with a jail cell in the back room."

Sheriff Garcia's lower jaw jutted out. "You may have missed the fact, Katie, but this place is a little crowded."

Ryan moved to Katherine's side. "I'm sure the ladies will cooperate for Elise's benefit. You wouldn't mind leaving, would you?" He waved a hand at the group.

The women chimed right in.

"Not a bit."

"Don't mind at all."

"It's late anyway."

They gathered their purses and paraded away.

Ryan laid his hand on Katherine's shoulder and gave it a soft push. "Why don't we sit and discuss this? I'm sure everything can be sorted out with a little patience."

She widened her eyes at him, lips pressed in a taut line. He pushed again. Her resistant body slowly sank onto the pew, and he sat beside her.

Lanette thumped down by Elise. She hugged the crying woman and glared at the sheriff. "Let's get it over with."

Garcia took a deep breath. "How much money have you raised?"

Elise lifted a moist face streaked with mascara. "One hundred thirty-eight dollars and fifty-seven cents."

"How much?" His hairy eyebrows crawled together.

Elise enunciated. "One hun-dred. Thirty-eight doll-ars. And fif-ty-seven cents!" She sniffled. "The change was from my granddaughter, God bless her. She wanted to help her Nana." Her voice cracked and got higher the more she spoke. "I wonder if they let children visit you in prison." She ended on a squeak and dabbed at her overflowing eyes.

Garcia rubbed two knuckles into the bridge of his nose. "Mrs. Walker, as I've said before, this is a friendly inquiry."

Katherine scoffed. "Doesn't feel friendly to me."

Ryan placed a hand over hers. If she kept this up, he might get the whole office to himself.

The sheriff glared at her. "Since the amount in question is so small, it can hardly be called fraud. Maybe petty theft."

Elise sobbed into a lace-edged hanky, and Katherine rose from her seat with a disgusted expression.

Garcia moved away. "I'm not saying she stole anything."

No one in their group spoke, but whispers sounded. Ryan saw a clump of people by the double doors. All eyes pointed at them. Who knew how many more were out in the parking lot on their phones? This ludicrous accusation was probably halfway to the city limits. He had to contain the situation before Katherine's temper exploded and earned her another notch on her reputation.

"May I make a suggestion?" He stood and angled his hip in between Katherine and the sheriff. "Since there isn't any indication of fraud, perhaps you could give Mrs. Walker a chance to search for her record book. She must have misplaced it. I doubt you'd consider her a flight risk."

Sheriff Garcia rested his hands on his gun belt and nodded. "Sounds okay to me. Elise, you go on home and look around.

Once you find it, bring it by the office tomorrow. Or Tuesday. Whenever it's convenient."

Katherine poked her head around Ryan. "Convenient? Like questioning her in front of the whole church? Was that for convenience?"

Garcia's bushy eyebrows lowered.

"Thanks, Sheriff." Ryan pushed against Katherine's forehead with his palm and stepped fully in front to block her from view. "We'll help Elise search and give you a call."

The barrel-chested man hiked his belt up, gave a nod to the women, and left.

Ryan rounded on Katherine. "Were you trying to earn yourself a night in jail?"

She glared at him. "This is no time to mince words. An anonymous coward is out to sabotage our campaign."

"Katie!" Lanette hopped from her seat. "Surely not."

Katherine crossed her arms in front of her. "Think about it. Your pictures plastered on Main Street. My pineapple-spiked smoothie. Elise falsely accused. We're being harassed so we can't make trouble for your husband."

Lanette shook her head. "Harry would never stand for such nasty shenanigans."

"No," Ryan said. "But it might be one of Mayor Johnson's supporters. Katherine has a point. There have been too many problems. It can't be a coincidence."

"What should we do?" Katherine turned to him.

"Keep our eyes open. Each attack has been different. There's no way to predict this guy's next move."

She grasped his sleeve. "That reprobate is no match for us. We'll catch him in no time."

Us?

A lopsided grin stretched across Ryan's lips. Since when was he part of the team? Katherine's unconscious slip-of-the-tongue informed him he wasn't on her suspect list. Not too long ago, he'd have been the first man she accused. His prickly neighbor was softening.

He had no business helping his rival. But dirty politics was bad for everyone. This wasn't personal. He was doing it for the sake of an ethical campaign. It had nothing to do with the woman beside him and her smiling green eyes.

Chapter Sixteen

K atherine squinted at the rows of figures on her computer screen. Math gave her a headache, but it didn't take an honors student to see the common sense in these numbers. If she could only get Lanette to deliver them in a clear way.

She bit her lip. Something felt off. A missing puzzle piece. Or was it nerves?

The unexpected crisis with Elise had monopolized their Sunday. They'd torn her house apart and found the receipts in the poor woman's knitting basket at two in the morning. Monday had been a red-white-and-blue nightmare, preparing the high school gym to Lanette's satisfaction. And now it was Tuesday.

Debate day.

What kind of questions would the moderator ask? Would Lanette be prepared or wing it?

A twinge hit Katherine's temple and burned a fiery trail down the side of her neck. She massaged the aching nerve. This didn't feel like an ordinary migraine. Could a political campaign cause a brain tumor? She drooped until her forehead pressed against her desk.

"Please, God." She stretched her arms forward, palms up. "I'm at a loss here. Help!"

The door creaked, but she kept her eyes pointed at the floral pattern of her desk calendar. She hated pink. Did Lanette have to decorate the whole stinking office in the wretched color?

"I've heard about the slower pace of small towns," Ryan's voice carried from the entrance, "but napping on the job?"

His footsteps drew closer. A bag dropped on the desk by her head. Delicious aromas wafted to the side of her nose not pressed against the calendar. Ryan's fingertips came into view as he tapped against the wood.

"I stopped by The Brunch Café. Susanna baked your favorite mint chocolate cookies. Some sugar might keep you from snapping at me all afternoon."

Katherine jerked up and grabbed the bag. The paper ripped in her hurry to open it.

"Take it easy." Ryan walked away. "I won't ask you to share."

She grabbed one of the cookies with the red-and-white crumbled candy baked in. The chocolate chips oozed in warm, succulent dots onto her skin. Katherine raised the sweet surprise and inhaled. The scents of brown sugar and peppermint danced through her nostrils.

Talk about an answer to prayer.

Katherine bit into the Heaven-sent treat and sighed. Thank God, Ryan knew her so well. He might be arrogant, but he knew how to pick a cookie. She liked that about him. Katherine popped the remainder in her mouth. It melted against her tongue in a rich, gooey blanket of deliciousness.

She liked many things about Ryan. His face. His height. His stylish but unfussy fashion sense. His ability to craft a witty reply to any question. The way he looked her right in the eye when they talked.

Katherine froze and stared at her empty fingers. A list of her officemate's positive attributes scrolled through her brain. Her gaze swung to his side of the office.

He straightened his desk, oblivious to her train of thought.

A frustrated huff left his mouth as he moved toward a folding chair. "Katherine, we agreed to share this workspace, yet I always find myself moving your junk." He grabbed a box of Lanette's campaign flyers and dumped it on the floor. Swiping a yellow sticky note, he scrawled on it. "It's been a while since I've had to claim my territory. Property of Ryan Park." He slapped the note on the chair. "Please keep your material on your side of the room."

Her lips floundered, but she couldn't make a sound.

"If your candidate insists on buying too much of everything, the least you can do is—" He took in her expression. "What? Don't tell me you finished a dozen cookies already."

Still no answer.

"Hello-ooo." Ryan waggled a hand in front of her. "Are you still in there?"

"Sorry. I just," she shut the lid of her laptop, "realized something."

He turned away and grabbed the cardboard box from the floor. "And what was this great revelation?"

"I," her chair legs grated against the tile as she stood, "like you."

"Of course, you do." He hefted the package. "How could you help but like an amiable fellow who feeds your sugar addiction?"

Katherine paused. He'd misunderstood her. This might be best. It wasn't too late to take the easy way out. Let him think she meant a normal good-natured affection.

But easy wasn't her style.

"No. I mean I *like* like you."

RYAN DROPPED THE BOX. The pointed corner landed on his toe, and he yelped. He bent and rubbed his foot for an unnaturally long time. No matter how he stalled, the proper response to Katherine's unexpected announcement eluded him.

He straightened. "You, you what?"

"Came as a shock to me too." A bemused smile lit Katherine's face. "You're emotionally closed off, and calculating, and I'm pretty sure you never say what you're truly thinking, but I like you anyway."

He gave a weak laugh and massaged the back of his neck. "Is this because I brought you cookies?"

"No use joking it away. You're so perceptive, you'd have noticed on your own."

Tick. Tick. Tick.

The grandfather clock on the wall counted off the awkwardness. This confession had come out of left field and socked him in the solar plexus. What should he say?

"And by *like* do you mean—" He waved his hand in a circle, unable to finish.

"Probably." She shrugged. "Guess we'll have to wait and see."

Was this a trick? Another attempt to rattle him before the debate? If so, it was working.

His eyes narrowed. "Aren't you afraid I'll use this against you? You've already categorized me as a heartless, calculating liar. Why would you like such a flawed individual?"

"That's not what I meant." She stepped around her desk and approached him. "Yes, you're clever enough to get around the difficult situations, but I can't recall hearing you utter one untruth, even though you work in politics. It must be some kind of miracle. You're honest. I like that. You're not afraid of me. I like that too."

He resisted the urge to retreat, but his nerve endings tapped an *SOS* against his skin. "Listen, Katherine—"

"And I like you because you call me Katherine."

"That's your name, isn't it?"

"Not to most of the town. You know I despise being called

Katie, and we've gotten into more than one verbal scuffle where you could have used it to spite me, but you didn't."

He scratched his cheek. How did he reply to this—this what?

It wasn't a proposal.

It wasn't a declaration of love.

It was just Katherine being Katherine. Saying exactly what she thought the moment she thought of it. The opposite of him. He admired her straightforward personality. In fact, there were many things to admire about her.

But he didn't plan to admit it out loud.

A romantic relationship between them was futile. Logistics denied him the possibility of considering it. She belonged in Sweetheart, and he was leaving in a matter of weeks. What was the point of starting something he couldn't finish?

Katherine stood a foot away, observing him. Waiting for his reaction. Ryan closed his eyes and sighed.

This was going to hurt.

Chapter Seventeen

Katherine barged through the museum door and collapsed on a stool by the cash register. Deanna swung around the counter like she'd stepped out of a 1950s housekeeping magazine with her perfectly coiffed hair and poofy black polka-dot dress. She held a pink feather duster at a picturesque angle.

"Hello, sugar." She tickled Katherine's stomach with the duster. "What's cooking?"

"My brain." Katherine cradled her head. "I may have, though it's possible I'm mistaken, but I doubt it—"

"Spit it out." Deanna ran the feathers along a glass display case of antique soda bottles.

"I think I've done something stupid."

"Sounds promising." She paused her cleaning. "Lay it on me."

"I fell for Ryan Park."

Deanna didn't move. Didn't say a word. Her head tilted ever so slightly. She threw her duster in the air.

"Hallelujah! It finally happened." She spun in a giddy circle. Her dress swirled, revealing a pastel green crinoline. Deanna seized Katherine, pulled her from the stool, and danced around the open space. "I'm over the moon."

"Why?" Katherine yanked away. "I'm not dating him. I said I like him."

"Sugar, I can count on one hand the number of times you've developed a crush. You considering a man in a romantic way is major progress."

Forget one hand. Katherine could count her crushes on three fingers. Her heart had always been slow to warm.

"I concede your point. But what do I do about it?"

"What every normal girl does. Get dolled up and do your best to catch his interest."

Katherine's shoulders slumped. The very suggestion pressed her down with the weight of an extra-large box of campaign flyers. She was terrible at flirting. Her straightforward personality balked at any kind of eyelash batting.

"I don't know, Dee. That's not really my style."

Her friend waltzed from side to side as a dreamy tune played through the overhead speaker. The crooner from bygone days sang with tender emotion. Deanna hummed along, grabbed a magnifying glass from the counter, and leaned close to Katherine's face.

She remained still for the examination. "Do you mind telling me what you're looking for?"

"I'm looking for Katherine Bruno. She's the confident, no-holds-barred, nothing-gets-in-her-way-once-she-makes-up-her-mind woman I've known my entire life."

She swatted her friend away. "Stop it."

"No, you stop it." Deanna planted her feet. "We've been friends since nursery days, and in all those years, you've never run away from a challenge. If you like Ryan Park, go get him."

"What happened to little Miss Old Fashioned? Aren't you the one always chastising me to behave with more decorum?"

"Sure. When it comes to everyday life and interactions with your neighbors, but Ryan's visit has an expiration date. If you don't make your interest known," the background music rose in a glorious crescendo of violins, "he'll return to New York, and you'll be left with nothing but what-ifs."

Katherine pointed at the ceiling and laughed. "Did you arrange the soundtrack? It fit perfectly with your speech."

"That singer declared his love with fanfare and a string section, but you should compose your own version."

"Love? I didn't say love. It's just," Katherine shied away, "admiration."

"Whatever." Deanna latched onto Katherine's arm and towed her toward the exit. "Admiration is still a good reason to share your feelings. Tell him."

"Stop shoving." She half-turned. "I already have."

"You told him?" Deanna grasped her by the elbows and whirled her around. "What did he say?"

"I didn't stay long enough to find out. He was standing there with his eyes as wide as silver dollars. Rejection was written all over him. I made some silly excuse about debate prep and ran out the door."

Deanna's focus traveled from the top of Katherine's lopsided ponytail to the tips of her scuffed white sneakers. "Please don't tell me this is what you wore for the big reveal."

She fingered the hem of her T-shirt. "And if it was?"

Deanna slapped her forehead. She got behind Katherine and pushed again, this time in the opposite direction.

Katherine swerved to avoid a rack of yellowed newspapers. "Where are we going?"

"To my emergency fashion stash. You're taller than me, but I have a black cocktail dress that will hit around your knees. We need to do damage control."

"What's the point? He's already seen me this way."

"Men are visual creatures, sugar. We want to make sure he understands what he's missing."

Even though the humiliated part of her wanted to turn tail and run, Katherine allowed herself to be railroaded to the storeroom door. Deanna was right. It wouldn't hurt to dress up a little. Now she'd accepted her crush, she didn't plan on burying herself in a hole. Might as well pursue it till the bitter end.

RYAN GLANCED at the clock on the office wall. Three hours until the debate. He typed one last statistic on Mayor Johnson's laptop and saved the document. It contained every speech, fact, and figure his candidate needed. Tonight would be the final nail in the coffin for Lanette Johnson's campaign. She had fought a good fight, but public sentiment in Sweetheart was too much in her husband's favor.

He placed his hands behind his back. It cracked as he stretched and twisted. A little longer, and he could leave this town behind.

A twinge of unforeseen emotion hit.

Regret? Surely not.

Sweetheart overflowed with charm, but he didn't belong here. It was time to rejoin the big game, with its lightning pace, excitement, and stress. The old familiar heartburn kicked in at the thought.

He rubbed the ache and looked around for his antacids. When was the last time he used them? With Katherine Bruno as an opponent, he should have swallowed a truckload. Had he actually acclimated to the small town's pace and learned to relax?

Katherine.

He stilled. She'd appeared confused as she'd admitted her feelings earlier. Confused and adorable. Like the revelation had sucker-punched her.

It must have been the cookies that made her so affectionate.

Ryan shook his head and laughed. Katherine was a passionate person who spoke without thinking. Chances were good she'd declare her hatred again when he did something else she didn't find worthy.

The door creaked behind him, and he froze. Act natural. The way his officemate had rushed out after her confession meant she'd probably pretend the whole thing never happened. That was fine with him.

Easier.

He swiveled his chair to find a beautiful stranger in the doorway. It took him five whole seconds to recognize Katherine. She wore a sleek black sheath dress with an asymmetrical neckline. Her makeup was subtle but elegant, and her usual ponytail was twisted into a sophisticated knot at the nape of her neck.

Ryan swallowed. He'd always known she was pretty, in a casual, uncomplicated kind of way, but now he realized Katherine Bruno was a knockout.

"Good afternoon." His eyes skimmed her outfit and landed on the sparkly pearl-colored toenails peeking out the front of her shiny, patent leather heels. "New dress?"

She gave a self-conscious tug to the slanted neckline. "A gift from Deanna."

"Looks good." He held up two thumbs. "Did you buy it for the debate?"

Her gaze raised to the ceiling, and she exhaled. "Not exactly." She turned to her side of the room and walked to her desk. "I dressed up to impress you."

She kept her back to him as she admitted it—her very fashionable, appealing back.

Ryan gave a short laugh. "Katherine, I honestly can't tell if you're joking or serious." He held up his arms in surrender. "You also said you *probably* like me, but what am I supposed to do with that? You're a truthful person. Still, I wonder if you're trying to get under my skin before the debate."

Katherine slid a ballpoint pen from her desk and clicked the top. She turned and stared for an interminable minute before moving toward him. Her high heels clicked against the tile, her steps steady and sure. She advanced as his personal space disappeared. Ryan retreated, and she followed until his legs were pressed against the side of his desk. He tensed, unsure of her plan.

Katherine raised the pen in her right hand. With her left, she swiped a pad of sticky notes from the desk—her attention never leaving his face. She scribbled, yanked off the first paper, and smoothed the yellow note on his upper lip. The outer edges peeled away from his skin, but it completely covered his mouth.

"What's this?" Ryan pushed his lips forward. His eyes crossed as he attempted to read it. Waste of time. He tried to remove it, but Katherine's slender fingers grabbed his own.

"It's a friendly reminder." Her words recalled their first conversation in the shared office. "I know how you prefer things clearly defined."

"And what are you defining?" The sticky note fluttered with his breath.

"My intentions."

She wrapped her free hand around the nape of his neck and pulled his head down. Without hesitation, she pressed her lips to the yellow note. The almost non-existent barrier protected his mouth from her actual touch, but the warmth of her lips transmitted through the thin paper.

Her slim fingers caressed the skin under his hairline for a brief second. She released him and moved away. He stared at her, his jaw drooping beneath the sticky note.

Katherine returned to her desk, grabbed her laptop bag, and winked. "See you at the debate."

She sashayed out. The front door closed behind her with a jaunty jingle. Passing the storefront window, she disappeared from view. Ryan plopped in his chair and stared at the wall opposite him. Had he dreamt the whole thing? He grabbed his collar and fanned it from his neck.

This was insane. She must be trying to rattle him. It wouldn't work. He was immune to any distractions. Nothing superseded the job. Miss Kiss-and-Run could forget about it. Not that he'd call the fleeting contact a real kiss. Not with a piece of paper separating—

The note!

He snatched it off his mouth and turned it around. Her message stared at him in bold capital letters.

PROPERTY OF KATHERINE BRUNO.

Ryan gulped.

Boom. Boom. Boom.

It took him a second to recognize the sound of his own heart slamming against his rib cage. It had been ages since anything besides a workout at the gym affected it, and he'd forgotten the sensation. Ryan dissected the unfamiliar rhythm. Was it shock? Annoyance? Attraction? Katherine was a beautiful woman. He'd have to be dead not to notice. And he certainly wasn't dead, as his still-pounding pulse reminded him.

Where were those antacids?

Chapter Eighteen

Katherine made it all the way down the street and around the corner before she collapsed against the side of Walker's Hardware Store. She pressed her palm to her mouth. Her heartbeat thumped inside her chest, setting a nice tempo for the accusation in her brain.

Wacko. Wacko. Wacko.

That must be what he considered her. Would Ryan call the sheriff for a restraining order? She couldn't blame him if he did. What kind of woman marked her territory with a sticky note and then sealed it with a kiss?

Katherine rubbed her lips. The square paper blocking her mouth from Ryan's had seemed a polite necessity. But frustrating, all the same. How did he really taste?

She hollered at the sky. "Did I make a bad move, God?"

Unless the gray clouds gathering over the building were a sign, the Almighty didn't answer. Katherine smothered a giggle. The look on Ryan's face. She should have taken a picture. They could show it to their grandchildren someday.

Grandchildren!

The idea set her high-heeled feet in motion. With every step, a new image flashed in her mind. Standing at the altar in a beautiful gown. Ryan carrying her across the threshold of the little cottage on Quincy Street. The kids playing in the yard with Bella and Romeo. First days of school. Mother of the bride. Grandchildren.

Her whole future passed before her eyes in seconds. Her whole future with Ryan. And it was beautiful.

No doubt about it. She meant to be Mrs. Katherine Park, although she'd launched her campaign in a questionable manner. Ryan appreciated straight shooting, so she gave him a barrelful. If her declaration of love-or-war meant he was a little rattled at the debate tonight? An added bonus. Katherine clip-clopped down the sidewalk with a smile. Even the sting of her toes in the too-tight, borrowed heels didn't ruin her mood.

How did Ryan feel? She couldn't be the only one who sensed a spark whenever they drew close. And they'd been more than close this afternoon, with nothing but a thin piece of paper separating their lips.

Had she been too pushy? Men preferred to make the first move. Right? Her impromptu kiss may have torpedoed any chance at a relationship with Ryan.

Remorse paralyzed her. She paused in front of the old Sweetheart Memorial Bank and braced a hand against the door's wrought iron knob. What if she'd ruined everything?

"Get it together." Katherine tapped her chest. "There's nothing you can do about it."

She straightened and nodded. Her cards were on the table. It was Ryan's choice whether to make a play or lock her out tighter than this old, abandoned building.

Katherine peered through the dusty window at the black-and-white tiled foyer and marble columns stretching to the vaulted ceiling. Such a waste. Of the building. Of her romantic potential. If only someone would give them both a chance.

She released the handle and headed for the museum where she'd parked her car. Tonight was Lanette's chance to show Sweetheart she was about more than decorating flower pots and organizing festivals. Once she laid the truth out in cold, hard numbers, people would acknowledge her capability.

"It makes no sense," Katherine grumbled. "Why spend fifteen million dollars on a new town hall when a beautiful building like the bank is sitting empty, waiting for—"

She tripped over an uneven crack in the sidewalk, whipped around, and stared at the carved wooden doors a few feet away.

"That's it!"

Katherine pointed a finger at the clouds above her, which had a definite silver lining this time. Was this divine inspiration?

"Nice one, God."

She released something between a laugh and a sob. She'd found her missing piece. Just in time to turn the debate on its head.

RYAN LEANED against the back wall, arms folded, and forced his attention away from Katherine on the front row. The warm copper highlights in her elaborate updo glinted in the fluorescent glare of the high school gymnasium. Her distraction technique had worked. She swirled through his brain like a barista drawing pictures in the coffee foam with a toothpick. At least the debate hadn't required too much concentration. In the expected style of Sweetheart, it was cordial and down-to-earth.

Mayor Johnson and his wife stood on the stage behind two lecterns. They'd talked about their love for the community and traded good-natured barbs in an old-married-couple fashion. The audience laughed a lot, but nothing earth-shattering had occurred.

He checked his watch. Ten minutes left. It appeared Harry's lead was in no danger. The moderator announced his final question regarding the new town hall, and the audience groaned.

Mayor Johnson nodded. "I know. I know. Y'all are sick of hearing about it, right?"

A few of the rowdier townspeople hollered in agreement. Ryan pulled out his phone and made a note. They should direct their last push toward a different topic to avoid wearing out the voters.

Mayor Johnson pounded a fist. "Me too. If I'd have known what a can of worms this would be, I might never have opened it. But what can I say? Sweetheart is the greatest little town in all of Texas. No, scratch that." He held up his index finger. "In all the U.S.A. and all the world."

A round of applause sounded.

"Sweetheart is the best, and I want the best *for* it, including the up-to-date architecture and technology that can usher us into the twenty-first century. I'm certain it will lead our town into a new era of prosperity and growth that will keep our kids here instead of moving to the big cities."

Whistles and foot stomping filled the gym as he gripped his hands above his head like a boxer and shook them.

Lanette stood at her own lectern, determination in her eyes. Ryan followed her gaze to the front row. Katherine gave her a nod, and Lanette's bright, red lips parted to show even, white teeth.

She dusted off the shoulders of her rhinestone-dotted suit jacket. "I love fancy stuff. Look at my fashion sense."

Laughter rippled through the room.

"I understand why Harry birthed this new dream. It's an honorable one. I'd much rather hold our Ladies Auxiliary meetings in a brand-new building with kitchen setups in every room so we don't have to run down the hall to reheat the coffee." She shook her head. "But the cost is too high."

Her husband jerked the microphone holder and cleared his throat. "We'll have thirty years to pay it off—nice and easy."

"Easy, huh? If everyone will please point their attention to my left." Lanette gestured to a large, portable screen.

Katherine rose from her seat and crouched beside the projector, connected to a laptop. She wobbled slightly in her high heels, and Ryan chuckled. What crazy plot did the two hatch this time?

A list of names flashed on the screen.

Lanette perched a pair of lavender glasses on her nose. "These are six towns across the U.S., from Florida to South Dakota, along with the cost of their city halls. They all contain similar populations as Sweetheart, and not one of their facilities costs more than seven million dollars."

The display behind her flickered as a fuzzy list of numbers appeared. Ryan squinted, but his stomach was already twisting in the shape of a Coney Island pretzel. At the front of the room, Katherine adjusted a dial on top of the projector. She gave her boss a thumbs up.

Lanette lifted a piece of paper and began to read. "A few years ago, Deer Park, Texas, a city whose population is six times the size of Sweetheart, built a new city hall."

A picture flashed on the screen showing the modern brick building.

"The price tag was five million five hundred thousand dollars, almost two-thirds cheaper than our proposed build."

The energy in the room spiked. People shifted in their seats. Voices buzzed.

"I bet you're surprised." Lanette nodded. "So was I. The cost per resident was one hundred seventy-seven dollars. A reasonable amount, I must admit. If our own construction was priced as such, I wouldn't be standing here before you."

The slide changed, and a single amount appeared on the screen. "But the projected cost of our new town hall is fifteen million dollars." She took off her glasses and grasped the top of the mic stand. "If this plan goes through, the cost to you personally will be one thousand thirty-three dollars a person."

Audible gasps filled the room, followed by murmurs.

"Our good citizens would give the shirts off their backs to

help Sweetheart, but why is it necessary for everyone to go around topless?" She waved at her husband. "If a bigger, more populated place than we are can do it for less, why can't we?"

Harry pulled a white handkerchief with a gold monogram from his pocket. He dabbed under his nose. "That's what the bill comes out to once we buy property and add everything we need. I only want what's best for Sweetheart."

"I know you do, precious." Her eyes took on a soft look. "There's no man in the state of Texas who loves his town more than you." She squared her shoulders. "But being sincere and being right are two different things."

The audience hooted and catcalled.

Harry opened his hankie and mopped his forehead, neck, and behind his ears.

Ryan resisted the urge to walk to the platform and snatch it from him before he swabbed his armpits. Did the man have to show exactly how flustered he was? Where did his wife get those numbers?

He knew without asking.

The small-town shrew had ambushed him again. An easy night had turned into a minefield. He typed on his phone but paused when Lanette spoke.

"Just like in marriage," she held up her left hand and waggled the finger with the gold band, "compromise is the solution. Harry's idea for a new town hall is wonderful, but why do we have to do things the hard way?"

She gestured at the screen as it changed to a collage of pictures. Ryan recognized the aged stone columns of the Sweetheart Memorial Bank on Main Street. Interior shots showed the tiled floor, thick carved staircase, and side offices.

"What you see before you is six thousand square feet, which already belongs to the town. The bank has sat empty for the past fourteen years, except for our occasional Christmas parties. I believe all of us can agree, this building has a grand, historic presence that fits the vibe of Sweetheart. We can hold community meetings and gatherings, purchase the modern technology my husband loves, and cut out the unnecessary expenses of land, architects, and construction."

Lanette turned her attention to the audience and clutched both sides of the lectern. "Harry and I have worked side-by-side to rebuild this town for the past sixteen years. We both want Sweetheart to succeed, but my way is better. Little by little, without signing our livelihoods away. If you elect me, I promise to make sure Sweetheart stays in the black. I'll also work at making those tourists who flood into our town once a year consider staying. If we bring in young families who want a safer, simpler way to raise their children, we can secure both the present and the future of Sweetheart."

Mayor Johnson visibly wilted under the pressure of his wife's eloquence. His chin jerked back and forth.

Ryan grabbed his notepad and scribbled with a black marker. He held it over his head for Mayor Johnson to read. The man scanned the message and nodded. When his turn to respond came, he walked out from behind the stand, moved to the edge of the stage, and stepped onto the floor.

He spread his hands out. "Fancy speeches aren't my thing. Never have been."

Sympathetic laughter answered.

"But I'm honest and hardworking. You know what to expect from me, which is saying a lot in this convoluted world."

Heads nodded around the room.

The tight line between Ryan's shoulders loosened.

Mayor Johnson took out his phone and waved it. "Every one of you have my private number and call it on a regular basis, because you trust me to help you. More than one person has said they feel secure with me in charge. That's why I want the town hall. It's another way to offer a voice to the citizens, a place where they can make their opinions heard."

He sat on the edge of the stage. "If anyone has a problem with the way I'm doing the job, I invite you to come up here and tell me about it. I've always been willing to listen." He clasped his fingers between his knees. "And that's all I got to say."

Many people clapped but not everyone. The moderator approached the microphone and thanked the crowd for coming. Chair legs scraped the floor as the audience rose to leave. Ryan tried to gauge their reactions. Some came forward to where Harry sat. Jud Watson slapped him on the back, but others gravitated to Lanette or Katherine. When he tried to count the numbers, it appeared to be an even split.

This wasn't good, and he knew who deserved the blame. He had to give her credit. Katherine brought the big guns tonight.

Chapter Nineteen

The radio blasted an empowered Eighties girl-band anthem as Katherine drove out of the high school parking lot and sped past the open fields. Ripened stalks of golden wheat glowed in the moonlight, and the world was beautiful. Poor Ryan must be out of antacids after tonight's embarrassing fumble by his candidate.

Victory tasted sweeter than a peppermint chocolate chip cookie.

For the first time, voters were starting to acknowledge Lanette as a viable candidate. People surrounded her after the debate. Mayor Johnson had stood off to the side with a grumpy expression, rattling his keys, and the couple left with six feet of space separating them. A few men stacking chairs remained in the gym as Ryan talked on his cell phone. Katherine waited for a chance to speak with him, but he continued the one-sided conversation without a pause.

Was he avoiding her? She supposed a public beatdown wasn't the best way to encourage romance. She should ask Deanna for help with tomorrow's outfit.

Beeeeeeeeeep.

Katherine glanced in the rearview mirror. A dark truck tailed her. The shadowy outline of a man in a cowboy hat sat behind the wheel. Why was this guy driving with his lights off?

She tapped her brakes to signal he could pass, but he stayed on her bumper. Idiot. What was his problem? It was a two-lane highway, but there was no one coming in the other direction. Blinding headlights glared in Katherine's mirror. She scrunched her eyes. Rolling down her window, she stuck out her arm and waved forward. The lights blazed closer, making no effort to pass.

"Go around!" she hollered.

No room to pull over. Deep ditches bordered the highway. If she hit her brakes, he'd plow into her bumper. She gripped the steering wheel and floored her accelerator. Could she outrun him? Her small sedan inched away. He caught up in seconds. The scenery blurred on either side. They raced at a breakneck pace.

Katherine checked her mirror. The glare blinded her. Nerves tightened. She looked at the road and squealed. A curve! She yanked the wheel. Stomped the brakes. Her tires skidded on loose gravel.

"Oh, God!"

No time for a longer prayer. Her car flew over the lip. It bounced down the embankment and hit the ditch.

Pow!

The air bag exploded. Her head hit the inflated pillow, lurched to the side, and banged against the door. The car shuddered. It settled at an angle as a dusty white powder hovered in front of her face.

Katherine coughed and rubbed her fingers over her nose.

"Owwww."

Was it broken? She grabbed the door handle and pulled. It opened with a creak and she stumbled out. Katherine scanned the road above. Not a sign of the truck.

She pressed a hand to her cheek. Cold sweat covered her. It slicked across her skin and oozed from her nostrils.

Oozed?

She examined her fingers.

The full moon illuminated dark red smears. Blood.

Her right high heel sank in the grass. Katherine kicked off her shoes and collapsed on the ground.

What should she do first?

Call a tow truck?

Find a tissue?

A steady beat pounded in her left temple. She kneaded the spot and prayed aloud.

"God, help me out here. And please let whoever that driver was get the biggest ticket of his life."

A motor sounded in the distance. Was someone coming? Would they notice her? She snatched her shoes and tried to scramble out of the ditch.

"Over here!" Her bare feet slipped on a slimy patch, and she slid backward. Hiking up the hem of her confining black dress, she tried again and reached the top as a silver SUV neared.

She waved both arms over her head, high heels in hand. Her neck jerked. The answering crack told her she might need a chiropractor in the morning.

The car slowed and stopped beside her. She bent as the passenger side window lowered. Ryan's shocked expression met hers.

"Katherine?" He stared. "What happened?"

She held her fingers over her bloody nose. "It's a long story ending with my car in the ditch."

"You ran off the road?" He threw his door open, leaped from his vehicle, and dashed around the front. His hands hovered over her arms as if he were afraid of hurting her. He scanned her body. "Are you all right? Did you call an ambulance?"

"I don't want to go to the hospital." Katherine rubbed her neck. "I'm okay. Just a little sore. Can I borrow your phone and call a tow truck? I left mine in the car."

He quirked a disapproving brow.

"Please?" she whispered.

Ryan hesitated. He drew the cell from his pocket and passed it to her.

She made a quick call to a mechanic friend, filled him in on the situation, and hung up.

"Twenty minutes." She passed the phone to him. "He has to finish putting his kids to bed, first. I can wait in my car if you want to leave."

His stone-cold glare told her what a stupid idea he thought that was. Ryan tapped the roof of his rental. "Why don't you stay here while I see what shape your car is in?"

"We may have to hold a memorial service." Her smile wobbled. "It was already on its last legs."

He opened the passenger side door. Holding her elbow, he gave a gentle push. "Sit here while I check for myself. Is there anything you need from the car?"

His consideration on top of the stress of the accident made the pressure build behind her eyeballs. She didn't want to break in front of him.

"M-my purse and," she cleared her throat, "whatever."

He considered her and reached in his pocket. Withdrawing a handkerchief, he pressed it tenderly to her nose. "Hold this. You look like you've gone ten rounds with a prizefighter."

She tried to laugh, but the vibrations shot tiny lightning bolts of pain through her cheekbones.

He disappeared down the embankment and returned a few minutes later with the skinny black clutch purse Deanna had given her. Walking behind his SUV, he climbed into the driver's side.

Ryan passed the bag over, grabbed the steering wheel, and angled his body in her direction. "How's the nose?"

He clicked on the overhead light and carefully moved her hand with the cloth away from her face. Placing careful fingers under her chin, he tilted it.

The dried blood above her lip crinkled on her skin. So much

for making a good impression. Why did Ryan Park have to see her this way? The one man in the world she wanted to dazzle.

"Is it bad?" she asked. As if she didn't know.

"The bleeding's stopped. There might be a bruise in the morning."

The warmth where his skin touched hers comforted the chaos in her brain. She closed her eyes and enjoyed the contact. She wasn't the type to play damsel in distress. But she might as well savor the tender moment.

RYAN EXAMINED KATHERINE, noting the pallor of her cheeks. His thumb stroked her silky skin. Did she go looking for trouble or just possess a talent for finding it? A car accident was no way to end an exhausting evening of debate. Not to mention her earlier —what could he call it? Romantic confession?

Common sense reasserted itself, and he withdrew his hand. Better to keep some distance between them. She might decide he was worried about her.

He *was* worried about her, but it might be best not to show it. No use encouraging her crush. That's all it was. A passing fancy. Once he'd left Sweetheart, she'd forget him in no time.

He turned his body away and leaned his head against the seat.

She faced the windshield and brushed the mud stains on her black dress. "Deanna's never going to loan me an outfit again. Thanks for stopping."

"Common courtesy."

The sound of their breaths dueled in the tense silence. Ryan shifted, flexing his fingers on the steering wheel and willing the tow truck to appear. Nothing, not even another driver, broke the darkness. He turned the key in the ignition and hit the button for the windows.

"Mind if I roll these down?"

She shook her head and dabbed at her nose with his handkerchief.

He killed the engine and viewed the purple Texas Thistle waving in the distance. The smell of late summer drifted through the car. Wild grass and flowers and a hint of rain in the air. A rattling squawk echoed.

Ryan tilted his head closer to the open window. "What's that noise?"

"Katydids." She lowered the cloth. "What you hear is insect speak for *Hey, Baby.* They rub their wings together in a kind of serenade to let the other bugs know they're interested."

Katherine flipped the visor and lifted the lid on the mirror. The small lights on either side cast a faint glow on her face. She dug in her purse, found a wet wipe, and swabbed her nose until every trace of red was gone.

Ryan watched from the corner of his eye, noting the way strands of hair had pulled from her elegant twist and curled in delicate waves around her cheeks. She looked softer, somehow. Vulnerable. Like someone should take care of her.

What was wrong with him? He needed to draw a line between the personal and the professional. Now.

He jerked his gaze to the side. "Did you write Lanette's speech?"

"Mostly. She told me what she wanted to say, and I added in the facts and figures."

He grunted.

"Why? Was it bad?"

"No. I hate to admit it, but she pointed out several relevant issues."

"Harry got a bit flustered but recovered in the end." Katherine snapped the mirror shut. "What was it you wrote on the notepad? I couldn't read it from where I was sitting."

Ryan chuckled. "Four words. *Show them your heart.*"

"Good advice." She nodded. "It's his strong point. What makes him such a good mayor. He truly cares."

"Then why are you working this hard to defeat him? Imagine the benefits the new town hall will bring to so many."

"So many?" she scoffed. "Population decline is a serious issue in Sweetheart. The kids go away to college and stay in the big city. If it keeps up, our town will wither away to nothing."

Ryan's brow furrowed. "Population decline?"

"It means when a lot of people start moving out of a specific—"

He waved a hand. "I'm familiar with the phrase. I'm just surprised you used it."

"I wrote a paper on the subject in college when I got my General Studies degree."

"I don't believe I've heard of General Studies."

She gave a self-deprecating shrug. "It's a buffet of courses for students who can't decide what they want to be when they grow up."

The corner of his mouth lifted. "And did you ever figure it out?"

"I've had twelve jobs in the past eight years," she spread her arms wide, "and now I'm the campaign manager and all-around gopher for the mayor's wife. What do you think?"

"I think you have commitment problems." He adjusted his seat and stretched out his legs. The rubber heels of his brown wingtips bumped the top of the brake. "Why so many jobs? Were you fired from all of them?"

"Believe it or not, no." She laughed. "I guess I kept searching for that zing. A sense of belonging. But it eluded me to the end. I wandered from job to job—feeling like the career equivalent of an old maid."

For the first time since they'd met, she was opening up. He kept silent rather than choose the wrong response, but Katherine didn't continue. The katydids amorous chirping highlighted the conversational lull.

Ryan checked his watch. Still ten minutes before the tow truck was due.

"What was your best job?"

Katherine didn't answer right away. Her brow wrinkled. "It floors me to admit it, but it's this one."

"Is it because you work next to such an attractive guy?" He poked an elbow in her side.

"Hardly." She returned the poke with enough force to leave his ribs aching. "It's ... interesting. Each day is different. Sometimes I interact with people, and sometimes I check the numbers. The variety appeals to me. The unpredictability."

"I admit you're not entirely inept as a campaign manager." He grinned. "You should keep doing it."

"Yeah, right. Sweetheart elections are few and far between. I'd starve to death."

"You could always move."

Her gaze focused past the windshield. "No." She gave a soft smile. "I couldn't. Sweetheart is home forever. My soul would shrivel up and die anywhere else. I believe God planted me here for a reason."

Ryan snorted.

"Are you mocking me?" She crossed her arms. "I know our small-town pace is too sedate for a big-city player such as yourself, but I think Sweetheart is great."

"So do I." He rubbed his stomach. "My improved digestion is living proof the simpler life has value. I just don't understand why an intelligent woman like you needs a religious crutch."

"Crutch?" Her brows lowered. "I don't get your meaning."

Ryan gestured at the crowded starry sky outside the window. "Do you really believe there's someone listening? Orchestrating where you were born and what your destiny is?"

"Yes." She sat straight up, turning the full force of her attention on him. "Don't you?"

He rolled his eyes. "I realized the fallacy of a loving God a long time ago."

"But," she reached out and placed a hand on his arm, "but

you said you were a preacher's kid. How do you go from mission trips to atheist? That's a huge jump."

"I grew up and stopped trusting in fairy tales."

She took a moment to answer. "When?"

"When the person who loved God the most didn't get her happy ending."

She searched his face. Weighing the new information. Realizing he meant every word. Her fingers released his arm. She twined them together and turned away—silent.

Katherine had opened her heart like never before, and how had he responded? By ridiculing her faith. Was he that desperate to push her away? Ryan steeled himself against the guilt. It was better this way. She'd get over her attraction quickly when she realized what a jaded sinner he was.

The awkward silence returned. Ryan tapped his finger against the steering wheel. The once roomy rental car felt about as wide as a shoebox.

Katherine's phone beeped twice before she checked the screen. "Al texted. He'll be here in a few minutes."

Ryan sighed. He leaned his seat back and propped his hands behind his head. "It's about time. I hope he can fix your car. How did you land in the ditch anyway?"

"Some idiot got right on my tail." She slapped the armrest. "He wouldn't slow down. Wouldn't go around. I got so distracted I didn't see the curve until it was too late."

"And he didn't stop?" Ryan lowered his arms and sat up. "Who was it?"

"I have no clue. Except it was a man in a cowboy hat."

He popped his seat into place. "What about the vehicle?"

"A dark pickup. Do you have any idea how many of those are in Texas?"

Ryan studied their surroundings. "Are there any cameras on this road that might have caught him?"

She laughed. "This is Sweetheart. Cameras would film an

unending cycle of local wildlife. We don't need those kinds of things."

"You needed it tonight."

"If I ever catch the jerk, I'll—"

"What if it wasn't an accident?" Ryan pointed at the trunk of her car sticking up from the ditch. "What if he meant to make trouble?"

"What?" She waved like she was shooing a fly. "That's crazy. This isn't the big city where you always have to check over your shoulder."

"Still."

A horn blared in the distance. The long-awaited tow truck pulled alongside, and a rotund man in black denim overalls and a red faded T-shirt with a hole in the collar hopped out.

"Hey, Katie."

She stretched across Ryan to talk to him through the driver's window. "Hi, Al."

Ryan caught a whiff of floral shampoo. A feminine scent for such a no-nonsense woman. Perhaps coming to her aid in a treacherous situation was playing with his mind. He clamped his jaw shut. They needed to talk more about this accident. During his political career, he'd witnessed all manner of dirty tricks. He wasn't the protective sort, but the sudden urge to shield her overwhelmed him.

She was no wilting violet. Katherine could take care of herself, but she didn't realize the danger she was in. There were too many accidents. Too many so-called coincidences.

Someone was targeting her.

Chapter Twenty

Bella and Romeo chased each other around the coffee table as Katherine polished it with an old washcloth. She hated dusting, but the act of wiping the furniture helped alleviate her desire to clean up her messy life. Too bad the clutter was in her heart, not her living room.

Ryan didn't believe in God.

The revelation floored her. She'd assumed from his background and moral character he was a Christian. Her faith was her foundation—the bedrock of her existence. There was no way she could spend her life with a man who didn't share her beliefs.

"Admit it, girl." She slapped the table with her dust rag. "It's not like he was beating down your door. It's better this way."

A romantic relationship between them had always been a bad idea. He lived in New York. She lived in Sweetheart. He worked for Mayor Johnson's campaign. She worked for Lanette's. Getting involved probably violated some sort of workplace code.

A knock sounded. Bella rushed toward it with a yip. Katherine made her way to the front door and opened it. Ryan stood on the porch with a white paper bag. His name-brand, black polo highlighted the matching sheen of his hair.

She clenched her fingers around her washcloth and said a silent prayer. All she had to do was keep her distance.

Simple.

Ryan shook the bag with a grin. "Have you eaten breakfast? I brought one of those apple fritters you always order."

Not simple.

Katherine squeezed her eyes shut. A gorgeous man who delivered sugary goodness without being asked. Why was this so difficult? She stepped to the side and jerked her head for him to enter. Bella spun in circles as he crossed the threshold. She pawed at his khaki-covered leg with tiny yelps of joy.

Ryan crouched to rub the puppy's ears. "I thought you only planned to foster the dogs for a month. Did you extend the commitment?"

She scuffed a bare foot on the carpet. "You might say that."

"Let me guess." He tweaked Bella's nose and straightened. "You signed a lifetime contract."

Why did he understand her so well? She'd agonized for weeks over giving Bella and Romeo back. The time and money required to raise two dogs didn't fit her lifestyle or her budget. Katherine had hardened her heart. She'd decided to pick the logical choice for a change and had made it as far as the animal shelter's front door, but one whine from the normally submissive Romeo had crushed her soul. It was game over from there.

Katherine ignored Ryan's grin and shut the door without comment.

His eyebrows dipped, and he studied her face. "I see your nose didn't bruise. How are you feeling?"

She rubbed her neck. "Sore, but I'll live."

"Do you need a ride to the office?"

"No thanks."

"Is your car fixed already?"

"No." Couldn't the man take a hint? She needed distance.

He leaned his head to one side. "O-kay."

Katherine wandered to the couch, pushed her laptop bag on the floor, and fluffed the pillows. She moved to the coffee table and wiped it with a half-hearted motion.

Ryan followed close behind. "What's this? Cleaning?" He lowered himself to the couch and set the paper bag on the table, pushing it her direction. "You should straighten the office too. It might score a few brownie points."

She swatted the bag away and rubbed at the polished wood. "It makes no difference to me how many points I have with you."

"You've changed your tune since yesterday." He leaned forward, arms resting on his legs. "I recall a certain person admitting how much she likes me."

Katherine stilled. Her gaze met his. That flirtatious twinkle made her want to throw the dust rag at him, but she restrained herself.

"I admit I felt a glimmer of attraction, but I realized it was hopeless."

"Hopeless?"

She nodded. "I don't date fools."

"Someone got up on the wrong side of the bed." He settled against the cushions. "Are we talking politics again?"

"No." Katherine moved to the other side of the room and attacked a layer of dust on top of the television. She breathed a little easier with a few more inches between them. "We're talking eternity. You said you outgrew the idea of God. If that's the case, we'd never work out."

RYAN'S SMILE FADED. He hated discussing religion. He should have gone straight to the office. What possessed him to offer her a ride? She obviously didn't appreciate the gesture. Her face radiated disapproval.

His lower jaw jutted out. "My belief system is different from yours. That doesn't make me a foo—"

"The fool says in his heart there is no God," she quoted.

He held up a hand. "Please don't pull out the scriptures. I've heard them all."

Katherine turned away and ran her cloth over the TV screen. "As I said before, I don't need a ride. Thanks for breakfast."

A frustrated gust left his lips. Had he really worried about hurting her feelings? She'd dismissed him like a piece of spam mail. What was wrong with her crossing him off her list anyway? He'd never wanted to be on it, but his competitive nature rose. It rankled that she found him unworthy.

He looked down, and her open laptop bag drew his attention. Yellow paper in the pocket. The corner of his mouth quirked as he reached inside.

Turnabout was fair play.

And he always played fair.

Ryan removed the pad of sticky notes from the bag, along with a pen, and wrote in large letters. He walked around the coffee table, stood in front of her, and held the paper for her to see.

An octagon with one word in the middle.

STOP.

Katherine squinted. "Am I missing something?"

"I read your message, loud and clear." He pulled the note from the stack and stuck it on her upper lip, so it covered her mouth. A familiar scenario. But this time, the roles were reversed.

His mouth descended until it hovered above hers. The paper fluttered as she gasped, and he yanked the note away. Katherine's eyes rounded. Quick, warm gusts of air brushed his lips as he spoke.

"Are you sure you want to keep it strictly business?"

Katherine gulped loud enough for him to hear. She barely nodded.

He stood motionless on the outside. Inside was another matter. Keep it in check. He remained a tantalizing one inch from her lips for three endless seconds before moving away.

"I agree." Ryan straightened his collar. "As I've stated from the beginning, let's keep things professional." He set the sticky note, paper, and pen on the table. "Since you don't need a ride, I'll be on my way. Have a nice day."

Chapter
Twenty-One

H ave a nice day?
Katherine stared at the door as it closed behind her tormentor.

Have a nice day!

How could she have a nice day when Ryan Park just blew her peace of mind to smithereens? The pulse pounding in her throat rivaled the beat of her favorite rock song. She forced herself to take two deep breaths. At least she'd affirmed she wanted to keep things strictly business. Right?

With a pathetic head nod. Zero conviction.

Had he noticed? From the quirk of his mouth—yes. The temptation of him standing so close had been too much to bear. A nod was all she could muster.

Katherine dropped to the floor and spread her body flat on the carpet like she was making a snow angel.

"Okay, God. If that was a test, I failed miserably." She flopped her arms and legs. "Why did you put such a sweet, gorgeous guy next door if you didn't want me to fall for him?"

Bella and Romeo sniffed around her torso as her brain dissected the last five minutes.

For the first time, she empathized with Mother Eve. Staring

at the shiny, delicious apple, or whatever kind of fruit it was. Dying to take a bite. Her entire life, Katherine had thought the woman was an idiot. An entire garden full of beautiful trees, and Eve hung out next to the only one declared off-limits.

Now Katherine understood.

She turned her face to the door where her own forbidden fruit had exited.

"Please, God," she whispered. "Just one little bite."

A tiny wet nose nudged her cheek. She raised her head and met Romeo's dark, soulful eyes. "What should I do?"

A shrill ring interrupted. Romeo bounced away with a yip as Katherine grabbed her cell from her laptop bag. Lanette's name appeared on the screen. She swiped the green button and held the phone to her ear.

"Hello," she moaned.

"Katie? Lands sakes, you sound terrible. Are you sick?"

"Yes." Katherine struggled to a sitting position. "I'm sick of Ryan Park."

"What happened? You two were getting along so well. Never mind. If you want to teach him a lesson, be at my house ASAP. I had a brainstorm."

Katherine shivered. The very word sent chills down her spine. If Lanette stayed true to form, whatever brainstorm she'd planned would be difficult and due yesterday. But it was the perfect excuse to avoid Ryan and the office. Good thing Lanette lived less than a mile away.

"My car's in the shop. I'll ride my bike over."

Fifteen minutes later, she sat on her employer's couch—ready to run home on foot.

"A rally?"

Lanette paced from one end of her floral living room to the other. "Yep. The kind you see on TV. Banners. Pictures. Balloons. And I'll stand on stage and inform the whole town about our plans for the old bank." She twisted her wedding ring on her finger. "There were plenty of people who missed the debate. We need to reach as many as we can. Don't you agree?"

"Absolutely." Katherine tapped her foot hyper-speed against the plush cream carpet. "But you want to hold it in three days. That's not enough time."

Lanette moved in front of her. "The election is in less than a week. We haven't a moment to spare." She whipped her bedazzled cell phone from her pocket and dialed. "I'll take care of the decorations. You contact the rental company about the stage."

Ding-dong.

Lanette jerked her thumb at the front door. "Answer that. Will you, honey?"

Katherine clamped her teeth and rose from the couch. "You're the boss." She exited the living room and turned left into the hallway. The bell rang again as she approached the entrance.

"Hold on!" she hollered.

Katherine grabbed the knob and swung the door open. The last person she wanted to meet stood on the other side. Ryan blinked at the sight of her.

She scowled. "What are you doing here?"

He held up both hands. "Not following you." Ryan edged past her. "I'm meeting Mayor Johnson in his study. Don't mind me." He waved as he passed the living room. "Morning, Lanette."

"Hi, handsome," came her cheerful reply.

Katherine stood at the open door, still grasping the knob. Was it possible her life could get any more wretched?

"Katie," Lanette called. "Let's get this rally rolling."

Apparently, yes.

A gentle breeze blew the willows in the front yard, and a bird's happy twitter beckoned. The flagstone walk lead away from the house like a yellow brick road. Her toes twitched inside her shoes. Should she make a run for it?

"Katie!"

She sighed.

No. Only cowards deserted in the middle of a battle. Katherine closed the door and returned to the living room with the air of a condemned woman.

RYAN MADE himself comfortable in the cushy wingback across from the oversized executive desk. The forest green plaid chairs provided a stark contrast to the rest of the chintzy house. Hunting trophies lined the walls, and a half-dismantled home gym sat in the far corner.

Mayor Johnson folded his hands on the shiny maple desktop and smiled. "I appreciate you coming here on such short notice."

"No problem." Ryan detected a pair of dark smudges under his candidate's eyes. "What can I do to help, sir?"

The man groaned. His shoulders rounded until they almost touched the desk in front of him. Above his head, a picture of his wife watched over them. Was it Ryan's imagination, or did she look disapproving?

"It's this way, son. I'm a peaceable man, and this election fight is draining the life out of me. Have you ever been in a situation so convoluted?"

"No." Ryan shook his head. "This is a first for me too. Frustration is natural."

"Frustration?" Mayor Johnson ran his fingers over his thinning gray hair. "I haven't had a decent night's sleep in a week. Isn't there any sort of compromise we could suggest?"

"Such as," Ryan raised a brow, "what?"

He leaned forward. "Is it possible to be co-mayors? Lanette and I were always a team. That way, she'd have an official title."

"I don't think it's the title she cares about."

"Makes two of us," he mumbled.

"Excuse me?" Ryan cocked his head.

"What does it profit a man if he gains the whole election, but loses his wife?" The mayor slumped in his seat like he was wearing concrete shoulder pads.

Ryan scooted his chair closer to the desk. "She might be angry at you for a few weeks, but she'll get over it."

"Even if I want to win, I don't enjoy beating her in public."

Ryan restrained himself from observing that was the whole point. Beating the opposition. Why couldn't Lanette Johnson bow out before election day and save them all a year's worth of stress? Then he'd pack his suitcase and head home to New York without a backward glance. His conscience pinged at the lie. The memory of Sweetheart would haunt him for a long time.

Along with a certain someone.

Ryan shook his head. Time to snap out of it. They had an election to conquer, and his candidate was wavering.

"Are you saying we should let your wife win?"

"Not in a million years." Mayor Johnson slapped his desk. Pencils rattled in the carved wooden organizer. "I just wish there was another way. None of this is worth anything without Lanette. I may have been mayor, but she and I built this town up together. Things were finally good. Stable. That's why I wanted the new town hall. To make a legitimate home where Sweetheart could do business—a symbol of security before I left office."

"Left office?"

"I'm not the political type, son. The reason I lasted so long was with Lanette's help. I'd much rather devote my retirement to fishing. If I can get the town hall built and turn Sweetheart over to a mayor who loves her as much as I do," he swiveled his chair to the picture of his wife, "loves her as much as *we* do, I'd prefer to spend the rest of my days as far from politics as possible."

An unsettled feeling burned in Ryan's gut. Antacids wouldn't help this one. It always appeared when something was wrong. His inner alarm, which served him well in the past. Trying to sell a candidate who didn't want the job was a fool's errand. But they couldn't stop now. The finish line was in sight.

New item on the agenda. Inject the mayor with the will to win.

A sharp knock, then Lanette burst through the door with Katherine close behind. "Don't mind me, gentlemen. I'm heading for the safe." She walked around the desk and shoved her husband's leg out of the way. "Move it, honey. I gotta get some cash."

"What for?" He scooted his rolling chair to accommodate her.

She ducked until only the top of her overblown blonde hair was visible. "My rally."

Six beeps sounded as she entered the code.

"Rally?" Ryan looked at Katherine.

She kept her gaze trained on her employer. Her lips frozen in a thin, unhappy line.

"Yep." Lanette pulled out a pile of folders and tossed them on the desk. "I need to inform the population of Sweetheart what I stand for. They might not come to a debate. But an outdoor show with music and barbecue and me making a short speech at the end?" She stood and waved a handful of bills. "That's a sure thing."

"Hold on a minute." Harry rose from his chair. "How much is this going to cost?"

"Oh, now you're worried about the expense?" Lanette rolled her eyes and walked out the door.

Harry scrambled after her. "Have you considered how much barbecue it takes to feed this whole town?"

Their receding voices argued until they faded away.

Ryan gave a tired laugh and rubbed his forehead.

"My sentiments exactly." Katherine finally acknowledged his presence.

"Are events in Sweetheart always planned in this," Ryan wiggled his fingers as if he was searching for the right word, "impulsive manner?"

"Whenever Lanette Johnson is involved." Katherine's weary chuckle matched his own. "My life will be nothing but decorations, errand runs, and late-night barbecue prep for the foreseeable future. You'll have the office all to yourself."

"Aren't you relieved?" He studied his wingtips and kicked at the green carpet. "Saves you the trouble of avoiding me."

She didn't answer.

He glanced up. "It's a shame. We struck a truce, and I had to go and spoil it."

"You didn't spoil it." Katherine turned away. "But our lives aren't headed in the same direction."

"God always did ruin my best relationships." Ryan stood and fiddled with a stack of papers on the mayor's desk. "What has He got against me?"

Her head whipped around. Katherine took a step toward him. Her green eyes focused with the intensity of a pair of emerald lasers. She studied his face as the silence stretched to an uncomfortable degree.

Ryan ran his fingers over the front of his black shirt. "What?"

A bemused smile lifted her lips. "You don't sound like someone who doesn't believe in God. You sound like someone who's mad at Him."

He held both hands in front of him. "Let's not start this again. If God existed, He wouldn't let such awful things happen. I refuse to waste any more time believing in fables."

"So, you admit it." She pointed. "You were a true believer."

Ryan turned to the desk and drew a pencil from the organizer. He twisted the yellow wood. "I don't want to talk about it."

"If you attended a seminary, your faith must have meant a lot to you."

Ryan remained silent. In his peripheral vision, he saw Katherine advance another step.

"Why did you stop believing?"

He slapped the pencil against the desk and faced her. "I stopped when the person who taught me about God died without warning. My mother went in for a simple operation, but an incompetent doctor took her from us." He lifted his chin. "She didn't have to die, but she did. That day, my faith died with her."

The room stilled, and the quiet stretched so thin he heard a faint ringing in his ears.

Ryan waited for her response. Perhaps a Bible verse. Or platitude stating the Almighty's ways were past their understanding. But she remained silent.

"What? No sermon?" The sound that left his lips was too bitter to be called a laugh.

Katherine's lashes swooped down. Her brows dipped in concentration. Her lips moved, but no sound came. She looked him in the eye and strode across the room with purpose until the tips of her shoes almost touched his own. Ryan would have retreated, but the desk stood in his way.

"What are you doing?" He noted a hint of moisture peeking over her lids and leaned closer. "Are you crying?"

"No." She sniffled. "Not really. I'm just so," she wiped her tears with her sleeve, "relieved."

Katherine threw her arms around his sides and squeezed. He froze, his own arms trapped against him. The warmth of her body pressed against his chest, and he forgot what they were talking about. He might have reciprocated, but her straitjacket hug prevented him.

Ryan rested his chin on top of her head. The confining embrace comforted him somehow. No one could ever call this woman predictable. "Dare I ask why you're relieved?"

"I just realized something very important." She released him and tilted a centimeter away. "You're not a fool."

He twisted his lips. "Thank you?"

"You're a prodigal." She beamed up at him.

"I'm a what?" He reared back.

"A prodigal. It's a story in the Bible about a—"

"I know the story."

"Great. Then you've heard how it ends." She moved out of

his space and headed for the door. "I look forward to the day when the Heavenly Father throws your welcome home party." She stopped on the threshold and turned with a wink. "I'll be the first one in line with a gift."

Her footsteps echoed down the hardwood floor in the hallway as Ryan stood paralyzed. If God did exist, He must have broken the mold and thrown away the blueprints when He created Katherine Bruno.

Chapter
Twenty-Two

K atherine wiped the back of a plastic-gloved hand over her cheek. Late afternoon sunlight warmed her body like a pastry in a toaster oven. The spicy tang of vinegar tickled her nostrils as she plopped another scoop of shredded pork onto an onion roll.

"Hey, Katie." Willy Walker lumbered by with two armloads of folding chairs. "Where do you want these?"

"In front. And thanks for helping."

"Sure thing. I may be voting for Harry, but I can't resist a good party. I even baked a few of my five-layer pecan pies to donate."

Katherine cringed. With less than twenty-four hours until the big event, she was grateful Elise had drafted her husband. He was the king of barbecue, but his pies were notoriously bad.

"You can put the chairs there." Katherine pointed at the large setup near the center of Sweetheart Memorial Park. A sagging stars-and-stripes sash on the small stage needed to be re-stapled, but the food prep came first. She studied the mountain of sandwiches in the metal pan beside her and growled. "Whoever invented political rallies should be hung by their thumbs over a pot of boiling barbecue sauce."

179

"To be fair," Deanna stood beside her in a navy dress and frilly red apron, spooning coleslaw into tiny plastic cups, "they usually don't feed people at these things. Uncle Harry had bottled water and mints at his."

"Candy's not good enough for Lanette." Katherine slapped another sandwich on top of the pile. "She wants every event to be a festival."

"Another reason why we love her." Deanna laughed.

"And why you're going to vote for her, right?"

She didn't answer.

Katherine's gaze cut over. "Right?"

Deanna stuck her spoon in the coleslaw and grimaced. "It's complicated. I told you choosing between Uncle Harry and Aunt Lanette was impossible for me."

Katherine pulled the gloves off and chucked them on the table. "Don't tell me you're not going to vote."

"Perish the thought." Deanna drew back. "That's unpatriotic."

"Then you have to choose. There are only two options."

"Not necessarily. I could put a random name where the write-in blank is. Abraham Lincoln. Harriet Tubman. Annie Oakley. They'd all make fine mayors."

"One problem." Katherine grabbed a new pair of disposable gloves from the box and slipped them on. "They're all dead."

"True." Deanna snapped her fingers. "I've got it! I'll vote for you."

"Me?" Katherine laughed. "Sweetheart would never elect me in a million years."

"Don't put yourself down."

"In case you've forgotten," she steadied the leaning stack of sandwiches, "I've offended almost everyone in town."

"You've got a mouth the size of Texas. I can't deny it." Deanna grabbed Katherine's arm and spun her around. "But we love you anyway, and I defy anyone to find a person who cares more about Sweetheart than Katherine Bruno. From the animal shelter to potholes, it's always you trying to make our home better."

Katherine's eyes stung. Why was she so emotional of late? The stress must be messing with her equilibrium.

She shook Deanna off and turned to the barbecue. "You're right. I'd make a great mayor."

If she changed a few dozen things about herself. Her temper. Her tongue. Her complete lack of schmoozing ability.

Deanna nudged Katherine's shoulder. "When Uncle Harry retires, you should consider running."

"Or when Lanette retires." Katherine took a box of plastic wrap and measured out a long transparent section. "How about I start with something smaller? Maybe town council."

"Great idea!"

"What's a great idea?" Elise Walker bustled to the table—her silver-gray hair swooped to one windblown side.

"Katherine has decided to run for town council." Deanna raised two fists in the air.

Katherine flapped the plastic wrap. "I didn't decide."

"Sounds good to me," Elise said. "Nobody ever wants that job anyway." She nodded at the stage. "Katie, I decorated Lanette's picture with the paper flowers. Now what?"

She pointed at a tray. "Carry those sandwiches to the taqueria. Rosa said we could keep them in the fridge overnight."

"You got it." Elise lifted the overloaded pan with a groan and left.

Deanna glanced at her silver wristwatch. "I have to scoot. I promised my mother I'd be home before dark. Sorry I'm leaving before we finish."

"Go." Katherine waved her away. "You've done more than your share."

It took another hour to finish the barbecue. Purple and coral tints of sunset painted the clouds as she tucked the plastic wrap around the last tray. She stretched and turned from side to side.

Katherine took in the orderly rows of chairs. A posterboard

picture of their beloved candidate sat on an easel at the front with paper mâché flowers framing the edges. Pink flags with the words "Bet on Lanette" flapped in the breeze.

"Katie!"

Katherine blanched at Lanette's bellow.

Her boss pounded across the grass, Elise scuttling at her heels. "Where are the flyers explaining our plan to convert the bank into a town hall?"

"They're in a box under the stage."

"No, they're not." Lanette swung her arm. "I checked."

"What?" Katherine's body tensed. "I know I left them there."

"Well, they're gone. If we can't find them, it's too late to print new ones." Lanette massaged her temples—her eyes clenched tight. Two fingers were missing their French tips.

Katherine stared at the imperfect manicure—a testament to the day's struggle. She couldn't remember another time when Lanette hadn't been exquisitely groomed. Garish taste in clothing? Yes. An over-fondness for pink? Absolutely. But still coordinated to the smallest detail.

"Do you need a drink of water?" Elise grabbed an empty cardboard carton from the table and fanned her friend.

Lanette looked up. Three tired lines gathered between her brows. "I need a way out of this mess."

Katherine stilled. Was Lanette bowing out of the race? A confusing mixture of relief and regret welled inside. She could finally get more than four hours of sleep at night. But what about the seven hundred barbecue sandwiches she'd made? More importantly, what about their plans Sweetheart? She'd started to believe the speeches she wrote for Lanette.

Katherine leaned her fists against the table. "What do you mean?"

"I mean, I'd quit tomorrow if my husband promised to shelve the town hall project, but I know that man. It's a matter of pride. Once he gets his ornery face on, he won't quit until the bitter end."

Elise sighed. "Men."

"You said it." Lanette pulled her buzzing phone from her pocket. "When Harry first ran for mayor sixteen years ago, I encouraged him. Not for the title or the glory. We did it for one reason. We love this town."

Elise rubbed her shoulder. "Of course, you do, honey."

"It took us forever to dig Sweetheart out of debt. I can't let him throw all those years of hard work away." She pressed the button on her phone and the screensaver appeared—a picture of Lanette with her husband bear hugging her from behind. A sad smile settled on her lips. "Harry's texting me. Making sure I'm okay."

"How sweet," Elise cooed. "Especially considering you spent last night at my place."

"You did what?" Katherine's eyebrows raised.

Lanette's mouth twisted. "Harry and I had a blowout. All we do is argue of late. So, I packed a bag and told him I was staying with a friend." A sob caught in her throat. "Forty-two years of marriage, and it's the first time I ever left."

Katherine walked around the table. "Nothing's worth wrecking your marriage. If things are that bad, you can quit the campaign."

"No." She gave a small, defeated shake of her head. "I can't let the town hall deal go through. It would break my husband to realize he'd harmed Sweetheart in any way. I refuse to let him suffer such a blow."

Katherine's jaw sagged. "Is that why you ran for mayor? For Harry?"

"Yes." Lanette dropped the phone on the table and ran a finger under her goopy mascara. "I don't want to be mayor. It doesn't pleasure me to put my family through this public brawl, but there's no other way." She raised a weary gaze. "Is there, Katie?"

Katherine glared at the screensaver shining from the table.

Harry Johnson's picture twinkled up at them without a hint of remorse.

Was love worth so much sorrow?

Ryan popped into her mind. Would she be willing to go through this kind of turmoil for a relationship with him? Katherine knew the answer without considering.

Yes.

No matter how much pain might be around the corner, she'd never be sorry she met him.

RYAN WOKE FROM A DEEP SLEEP, stretched his arms wide, and repositioned the couch pillow under his head. Just beyond his legs, the bright red numbers on the digital clock told him it was late. He couldn't remember the last time he'd taken a three-hour nap. In New York, his brain barely allowed him to sleep.

He hadn't used his antacids in weeks. He should be chewing them like peanuts with only two days left until voting. Was Sweetheart some kind of enchanted stomach soother?

His latest poll confirmed his suspicions. Lanette's approval rating had grown, but Harry was still in the lead. People preferred the familiar over taking a chance. Unless the ladies' barbecue sandwiches worked miracles at the rally tomorrow, it was too late for her to catch up.

He rose from the couch and padded to the window in his bare feet. Drawing the curtain aside, he took in the starry sky sparkling through the oak branches in the front yard.

Was Katherine home yet?

She'd used her bicycle since the accident. Perhaps he would drive over to the park and offer her a ride. He grabbed his keys from a bowl by the door and slipped his feet into a pair of sneakers. He'd reached the top of the porch steps when a whir of spokes alerted him to his neighbor's arrival.

She rode her bike up the driveway. The old metal frame

creaked as she stopped. Katherine dismounted and propped the kickstand in place.

"Evening," Ryan said.

She jumped at his voice. "What are you doing up?"

"I was worried about you."

"Really?" Her face softened in the glow of the porch light. "I'm not used to having anyone watch out for me."

"And I'm not used to having a neighbor who attracts trouble like a magnet."

Her pleased expression disappeared. "I don't go looking for it. But things happen."

"Did anything happen today?" Ryan made his way down the steps and met her at the bottom. A cool breeze rustled through the tall trees surrounding the duplex.

She avoided his eyes. "Nothing too terrible."

Ryan moved into her line of vision. "But something happened?"

Katherine grimaced. "A box of flyers disappeared. I put them under the stage, and they aren't there now."

"What kind of flyers?"

"They explained Lanette's alternate plan for a town hall."

"You mean your alternate plan." Ryan pointed a finger at her. "Let's give credit where it's due."

Katherine ignored the praise. "Anyway, they're gone, and the printshop was already closed. Lanette will have to spell out the details in her speech."

Ryan crossed his arms. "I think your saboteur struck again."

She bared her teeth. "If I ever find out who it is, I'll—"

"This guy fights dirty." Ryan placed a hand at her back and pushed her toward the stairs. "If he tries anything else, let the sheriff handle it."

Katherine skidded to a stop. Her body resisted as he attempted to nudge her up the steps. "What else would this jerk try?"

Ryan wanted to kick himself. Why did he plant the idea in

her brain? He should have let her go in the house. Or offered to cook her dinner.

"You must be hungry." He gestured to his place. "I've got steaks in the fridge."

"What. Else?" Her chin jutted out.

Ryan blew air through tightened lips. "He probably took your flyers. Now your whole rally setup is sitting unguarded. I realize that's the Sweetheart way. You leave possessions out and expect them to be in the same place the next morning. But what's to prevent him from sneaking to the park and tearing things up?"

Her eyes widened. "You're right."

"I suggest you call the sheriff and ask him to have a deputy drive by a few times during the night."

Katherine didn't answer. She stared off in the distance. The corners of her mouth lifted.

Ryan ducked his head to take a closer look. "Dare I ask why you're smiling?"

Katherine grinned. "Because this is a golden opportunity to catch the weasel."

The wind kicked up. Clouds blew across the moon, casting a shadow on the front yard. Katherine dashed to her bicycle, straddled the seat, and released the kickstand.

Ryan rushed after her. "Am I correct in assuming you're going to the rally site?"

"Yes."

"Looking for trouble?"

"No." She raised her nose. "Answers."

"By yourself?" He thumped the handlebars. "Do you think that's wise?"

"I think it's the perfect time to figure out who's targeting Lanette's campaign. If I were the saboteur, I'd wait till people left and then rip it apart." She placed a foot on the pedal.

"And what if you're right?" He moved in front of the bike.

"Let's say you catch the culprit messing with your setup. Will you confront him by yourself?"

"I'll call the police." Katherine pulled a small can from her pocket. "And I have pepper spray if I need it."

"Which means you *will* confront him." Ryan gritted his teeth. Did this woman have no self-preservation instinct?

She tried to maneuver around him. "Whoever this idiot is, he needs to be brought to justice. I refuse to let him destroy my hard work without any consequences."

The clouds moved, and a shaft of moonlight highlighted the obstinate set of her jaw. Ryan ran both hands through his hair. "Okay."

Katherine hesitated. "Okay." The cheerful note in her voice sounded a bit forced. "See you later."

Pushing off, the bicycle moved a foot before he seized it by the rear rack. "I meant, okay, I'll go along. Give me a minute to grab my phone."

Katherine tapped her bike. "Are you driving?"

Ryan smirked. "Unless you want to ride double."

An image flashed in his brain—Katherine pressed against him while he pedaled. Her arms wrapped tightly around his body. He stepped on the mental brakes. This wasn't a scene from a romantic comedy. They were going to trap a criminal.

From the bemused set of her mouth, Katherine must be imagining a similar scenario.

"Forget it." Ryan slashed his arm through the air. "Put your bike away. We'll take my car."

He ran up the steps, entered his half of the duplex, and blew out a long breath.

Focus. It was time to catch a pineapple-pushing, flyer-stealing, tailgating creep.

Chapter Twenty-Three

A Texas-sized moon crested high in the sky as they parked by The Brunch Café and walked to the park. Heavy air hung around them in a humid curtain, and the buzz of katydids hummed in the trees. The streetlights from the nearby parking lot illuminated the edges of the rally setup, but the stage was shrouded in darkness.

Ryan strode down the middle aisle between the folding chairs. "We should—" he paused. "Where are you?"

"Here." Katherine jogged over from a side table, clutching a canvas bag. "I was just fixing something. Where do we wait?"

He made a slow circle around the rows of chairs. "Not out in the open. This guy plastered Lanette's pictures all over town when no one was around. It has to look deserted, or he'll never appear. That's why we left the car around the corner."

Ryan studied the perimeter. Not a sign of movement.

"I've got an idea." Katherine pointed at the children's playground about twenty feet behind the stage.

She grabbed his sleeve and pulled him with her. They stopped underneath the elaborate cedar swing set with a long green slide and a miniature house.

Katherine ducked her head in the small-scale wood cabin. "We can hide in here."

She dropped to her knees without waiting for a response, crawled inside, and scooted her body around by the window cutout on the right.

Ryan followed. The smooth wooden boards brushed against his palms as he took the spot by the matching window on the left. His head bent over his knees in the tiny space.

"I may need physical therapy after this," he griped.

They sat side by side in total silence. The occasional roar of a car engine carried through the night from far away. Ryan scanned the area, listening for any sign of an intruder.

Table skirts swished in the wind. The ancient oak trees stood stark against the starlit sky, and a lone owl hooted from one of the branches. Five minutes passed without so much as a stray cat wandering by. Were they wasting their time?

Ryan heaved an exaggerated sigh.

Katherine shifted his direction. She was no more than a silhouette in the unlit playhouse.

"You didn't have to come," she whispered.

"Yes, I did." His low tone matched her own. "It will prove once and for all it isn't me messing with your campaign."

"I know it isn't you." She poked his leg with her toe. "You're not that kind of person."

An unexpected pride welled inside. He used to be number one on her list of suspects. Her unequivocal vote of confidence had been hard to earn but worth it.

Ryan breathed in the balmy air. His insides, once tight as a bed coil, relaxed in the priceless simplicity of a Sweetheart summer evening.

"If you ever follow up on your plans to bring new visitors to Sweetheart, be sure and highlight the natural beauty—the trees, the wildflowers, the fishing lake. But also list the many places available to charge their cell phones."

She laughed like he'd hoped she would. "Do big city types enjoy this kind of thing?"

"The novelty of tasting fresh unpolluted air and seeing more than three stars in the sky tickles their fancy. Plus, the scenic photo-ops."

"I don't know. They might find it dangerous here."

"Dangerous how? You mean wild animals?"

"Hardly." Katherine waved a finger at the sky. "There's something about staring into a star-laden expanse that releases your inhibitions. Makes you want to unburden your soul. You end up confessing all sorts of secrets"

His eyes adjusted to the darkness, and he began to make out her features. "If you feel inclined to share, lay it on me. Especially any campaign strategies."

"If it weren't for you, I wouldn't have to be making strategies."

"How do you figure?"

"If Harry hadn't hired you, Lanette wouldn't have drafted me."

Ryan chuckled. "Drafted is the perfect word. If she hadn't roped you into this political three-ring circus, where do you see yourself?"

"What?"

"Those twelve jobs in your past. None of them gave you that zing. What do you really want to do?"

Katherine turned away. "You'd never believe it."

"Too shameful?"

"No. Too ordinary."

She paused so long it seemed she wouldn't continue.

Ryan waited. You couldn't push people to share their secrets, or else they'd give you the edited version or outright lie.

Katherine twisted her fingers. "There's a small cottage on Quincy Street. My mother and I used to walk past it on the way to school. I remember telling her I was going to live in it someday when I was a mom. That's stayed my dream for over twenty years. Find the right job. Buy my cottage. Get married. Raise a family."

"What's wrong with raising a family?"

"Nothing. But the people in this town think I'm a no-holds-barred, independent harpy. Very few men are brave enough to ask out that kind of woman."

He couldn't argue with her logic. But as she pushed a strand of silky brown hair from her averted face, she looked anything but the foreboding shrew. What was wrong with the men in Sweetheart? Didn't they realize what a catch they were missing?

Vibrant. Caring. Beautiful.

Risky thoughts. He cleared his throat.

"Here." Katherine dug in her bag and tossed him a water bottle.

Considerate.

He should add that to the list. Katherine Bruno had a lot going for her. It was a shame she couldn't see it. He twisted the cap off the bottle and raised it to his lips.

Katherine cupped her hands around her mouth and whisper-shouted. "God!"

Ryan froze with a mouthful of water.

She waved a fist at the sky. "Why is it taking so long?" She thumped the wooden floor. "Other people get all the regular stuff without even trying. Why don't I?"

Was she asking him? He swallowed, but she spoke before he could answer.

"God, are you there? I'm not requesting a personal visit from Gabriel. Just any kind of response."

Wasn't she embarrassed? It made no difference he was sitting across from her. She spoke to God like the Almighty was in the same room. Had he ever been so unashamed?

"What makes you think He's listening?" Ryan took another drink of water. Keep it casual. No sense encouraging false hope he might be softening.

"Of course, He's listening."

"How can you be so sure?"

Deep down, he truly wanted to know. Katherine Bruno wasn't naive or easily fooled. How could this sharp, discerning woman trust wholeheartedly in a Higher Power?

A soft hoot echoed from the darkness.

She inclined her ear to the window. "Hear that?"

Ryan nodded.

"The Bible says He cares when a tiny sparrow falls, and I'm worth so much more to Him than a bunch of birds."

"And fairy tales always end with happily-ever-after." Ryan altered his position to stretch his legs from one corner to another. "It's a bunch of soft-soap lies to help humanity cope with its sorry lot."

"Sorry?" Katherine scooted his way until she was right beside him. "This big, wide, wonderful world is beautiful and messy and exciting and, yes, heartbreaking. I don't know why so many sad things happen. I don't know why I lost both my parents on the same day to a drunk driver. But I can't deny there's a God when I see Him in the beauty surrounding me." Her shoulder knocked against his as she crossed her arms. "Perhaps He's easier to ignore where you're hemmed in by skyscrapers and concrete. Out here, you can feel Him."

"Even if I conceded your point," Ryan picked at his sweatshirt, "it doesn't mean He cares about us."

She uncurled her legs beside his and crossed her ankles. "I guess that's where faith comes in. People are quick to blame God for the horrible things, but do they give Him equal credit for the good stuff? Little miracles are all around."

"Are you trying to save this sinner's soul?" Ryan cocked his head. "Should I pass the offering plate?"

"Wait till I finish my sermon." She bumped his arm with hers. "I think there are two ways to react to tragedy. You can run *from* God or *toward* Him. You chose the first. I chose the second."

"I suppose you're going to tell me your way was the best. God made everything better."

"Khhhhhh." A puff of air left Katherine's mouth. "I do believe choosing God is best, but my problems didn't magically disappear. My mom and dad were still dead. I went from cherished only child to living with an uncle who treated me like I was invisible. I thought God took away my perfect life, and I reminded Him for three years. I hollered, and raged, and cried my eyes out as I asked Him why He let it happen. Why couldn't—"

She halted. The breath stuttered from her nose. Several seconds passed before she continued. "Why couldn't it have been someone else's parents?"

Her quiet agony called to him. It echoed the grief-filled questions he'd railed at Heaven after his own mother died. Burning spread through Ryan's gut. He blinked and squinted at the starry vista outside the window.

Katherine drew her knees up and hugged them. "The bitterness ate me alive. I remember one night I didn't sleep at all. At dawn, I walked to the pond on my uncle's ranch. The sun was rising over the tree line. Springtime. Texas Bluebells surrounded the water. The birds sang. The air smelled clean and new, and I longed for that same kind of fresh start in my soul. I told God I didn't understand, might never understand, but I was grabbing on to Him and holding on with both hands for dear life. If He wanted to let me in on why He allowed my parents to die, I'd be willing to listen. But if He didn't, I was still going to stick with Him."

Ryan looked over at her. "Did He ever answer you?"

"No." She laughed. "At least, not with words. But a small seed of peace sprouted in my soul. Little by little, it grew until, one day, I realized I wasn't bitter anymore."

He envied her. How would it feel to live the same way? Free from his acidic longing for a past that was gone forever.

Anguish shot up inside him—forceful and heavy like a geyser. A sharp pain in his cheek told him he was clenching his teeth. He relaxed his jaw, and the words spilled from his lips without permission.

"I miss her—my mom. Every day."

She sniffled beside him. "I know." Her silky head dropped onto his shoulder, heavy and warm and comforting. "Maybe we—"

A twig snapped.

"Shh." Ryan covered her mouth. He pointed with his chin at the outside, slowly released her, and they both stared into the black night.

A small glare from a flashlight shone in the distance. It traveled from the parking lot and made its way through the rows of chairs. A large person held it. From his build, it was a man.

Ryan searched for his phone. Should he record this?

No. If the man spotted the screen glow, he might run. And they still couldn't tell who it was. The figure drew closer to the stage. He wore a ball cap low on his forehead, a puffy black jacket, dark jeans, and cowboy boots. His movements were slow but assured. Arrogant. He didn't crouch or hide on the outskirts.

The stranger's footsteps pounded in the stillness of the park. Ryan laid his hand on top of Katherine's. It trembled.

A clicking sounded.

Once. Twice. Three times.

Followed by a hiss and a crackle.

The scent of smoke reached his nose. A small flame appeared near the stage. Katherine jolted.

Ryan shoved her down. "Wait here."

He slipped from their hiding place, a few feet from their target, closed the distance between them, and grabbed the man.

Jud Watson spun and hollered. A cigarette dangled from his lips, his face illuminated. Flames engulfed the giant picture of Lanette. Paper roses lit in fiery puffs and crinkled into black charred balls.

Ryan gripped his arm.

The man yelped.

Katherine joined them and gasped. "Jud!"

"Katie?" He looked wide-eyed at her and Ryan. "Quick! Get help!"

"What?" Her brow wrinkled.

Jud yanked off his ball cap. "Don't just stand there, girl. This whole place might go up like a tinder box."

She dashed to a table and pulled a portable extinguisher from underneath. Ryan stood opposite Jud, fists at his side, ready to tackle the man if he tried anything.

He didn't.

Jud waved his phone. "I'm calling the fire department."

Whatever game this creep was playing, Ryan didn't have time to analyze it.

Katherine rushed toward the fire.

Ryan yanked her away, took the heavy extinguisher, and pulled the safety pin. The lever clicked as he squeezed. A yellow cloud shot out. It swept over the burning poster. The wind flung the chemical dust in every direction. It blew in his nostrils and choked him.

The flames died.

As the smoke cleared, all that remained of Lanette's photo was her right eye and half a blonde bob.

Ryan dropped the extinguisher and covered his mouth with the arm of his sweatshirt. A hacking cough shook his body. He bent over and cleared his throat, spitting on the ground.

Katherine pounded him on the back. "Are you okay?"

He coughed. "Stop beating me, and I'll check."

She rubbed his arm. "Do you want me to call an ambulance?"

"Already done," Jud declared.

Ryan and Katherine turned to the forgotten perpetrator. He stood with his hat in one hand and his phone in the other, the cigarette still in his mouth. Jud raised the cell. "They're on their way. It's good you two were here. I would have felt awful if something happened to Lanette's party."

Katherine advanced. "Then why did you try to burn it down?"

"Try to—" He rubbed his bearded chin. "What do you mean, Katie? You don't think I did this on purpose, do you?"

Ryan moved in between them. "You have to admit, Jud, it looks suspicious. What are you doing in the middle of the park at three in the morning?" He waved at the man's outfit. "Dressed like the villain from a crime drama?"

He gave a tug to his jacket. "I been having trouble sleeping of late. Comes with old age. I reckoned a walk might help."

Katherine shoved past Ryan. "Your ranch is ten miles outside of town. Don't tell me you walked that far."

Jud's jaw hardened. "I was spending the night at Wilbur's. You can check with him. He lets me crash on his couch when there's a big event going on. I wanted to be here bright and early for Lanette's shindig."

The harsh wail of sirens pealed. A long, red truck raced into the parking lot. The square filled with firemen, EMTs, and Sheriff Garcia.

"Shoot." Jud scrunched his face into a mass of wrinkles. "I feel bad getting everybody out of bed at this hour."

Ryan scrutinized the older man. He seemed chagrined, but not nervous. Shouldn't an attempted arsonist betray more guilt?

Could this really be an untimely coincidence?

Chapter
Twenty-Four

The remnant of Lanette Johnson's torched campaign poster shuddered in the breeze. Her one remaining eye stared in judgment upon the man who was crushing the stub of his cigarette with a booted heel. Katherine folded her arms over her stomach. If Jud believed she bought his pathetic excuses, he was dumber than a bucket of rocks.

"Are you saying you accidentally set fire to Lanette's picture?"

"I got the craving for a cigarette." He glanced at the charred debris and winced. "Wilbur doesn't smoke, so I always have to go out of the house. The lack of sleep must've made me punchy. I tossed the match away, and it hit the poster. Before I knew it, the whole thing went up in flames."

The sheriff sauntered over, tucking his shirttail in his waistband. "Got your message, Jud. What happened?"

"It's my fault, Garcia." Jud hit a palm to his forehead. "My smoking just about killed more than me for a change. I gotta quit those things." He focused on Ryan and Katherine. "I'm sorry, y'all."

Garcia scratched his barrel chest. "Anybody injured?"

"No, thank goodness." Jud answered before anyone else

spoke. "I couldn't have lived with myself if Katie or Ryan were hurt."

Garcia patted Jud's shoulder. "How about you let the EMT check you over?" He led him away to the waiting paramedics.

Katherine scoffed. "Do you buy any of his guff?"

Ryan rubbed his throat. "It's hard to say. I wish this town had security cameras."

"Wish granted." Katherine snapped her fingers. "Follow me." She dragged him to a decorated table and pulled her phone from between the flower arrangements. Katherine triple-tapped the screen, and the display turned on.

Ryan leaned in. "Are you telling me you left your phone recording this whole time?"

"Yep." She stopped the camera. "I hope this angle captured Jud with the poster. It was right next to where he stood. Once I check the footage, we can prove whether or not Mr. It-was-an-accident is telling the truth."

"Hey, you two!" Sheriff Garcia shouted from beside the ambulance. "Come over here and get checked out."

Katherine waved at him. "Give us a minute, Sheriff." She mumbled a quick prayer. "Please, God. Let the video provide the proof."

She scrolled to the last five minutes. Ryan drew close as they both watched. Jud appeared from the side and passed right in front of the camera. He walked deliberately to the poster. A clicking hiss and then a tiny flame.

"Did you hear that?" Katherine turned with a triumphant smile just as Ryan looked at her. Nose-to-nose, her brain short-circuited, and she forgot what she was going to say.

He grinned. "That was no match."

"Huh?" She stepped away. "Oh. Right. More like the spark a lighter makes."

"My thoughts exactly." He placed a hand on the small of her back. "Let's show the sheriff."

Two glaring lights from the ambulance illuminated the

parking lot. Sheriff Garcia talked to his deputy as Jud Watson sat on a stretcher with an oxygen mask covering his mouth and nose. The EMT made a note on his clipboard and climbed in the front seat of his rig.

Jud removed the silicone piece as they approached. "Are you two okay?"

"Better than you." Katherine held her phone in front of her. "After the sheriff sees this."

"Sees what?" Sheriff Garcia turned their way.

He joined them beside the stretcher. Ryan took the spot at Katherine's elbow, between her and Jud.

"Katie!" Lanette's voice pierced their huddle.

She rushed to their group, her husband right behind. Her boss wore a leopard print tracksuit, and her hair was wrapped in a pink scarf.

"Harry got a call about the fire and texted me. Are you hurt?" She pushed Katherine one way then the other as she checked her over.

"I'm—" Katherine brushed her away. "Stop. I'm fine. And I recorded video on this phone." She waved her cell in the air. "It proves Jud didn't accidentally toss a match near the poster as he claimed. It was a lighter, and he did it on purpose."

"On purpose?" Lanette's makeup-free face sagged.

"Jud!" Mayor Johnson pushed between Ryan and the stretcher. "There's no way that's true."

Jud's gaze darted from the mayor to the sheriff. "I got a little confused in all the excitement. I was using my lighter, but it was still an accident. This girl's off her rocker."

Katherine moved at him, but Ryan grabbed her elbow.

He stepped in front of the man and spoke in a conversational tone. "It's an easy mistake to make. A stray spark from a cigarette lighter. The wind blowing the poster nearby."

"Yeah." Jud nodded at him. "A mistake."

Katherine jerked her arm from Ryan's grasp. "You must be kidding."

Hurt and anger swirled in a dismal vortex. He wouldn't betray her this way. Although they were on opposite sides, he'd always been an honorable opponent.

"Ryan?" Every cell in her body begged him not to disappoint her.

His polite facade stared at her without emotion, but his eyes said something different. Trust him. It went against everything in her nature to leave it alone, but she bit her tongue and took a step back.

Ryan slapped Jud's shoulder. "I haven't been in Sweetheart long, but I've seen what an influential member of the community Mr. Watson is."

Jud's chest puffed out. "That's right. Influential."

"We've been friends for sixty years," Mayor Johnson confirmed.

Sheriff Garcia tipped his hat on his forehead and crossed his arms.

Ryan took a blanket from the end of the stretcher and draped it around Jud. "Mr. Watson would never commit arson. Or spike Katherine's drink with the pineapple she's allergic to."

"Never." Jud's chin bobbed like a fishing lure.

"I saw him across from the campaign office on the night those defamatory pictures of Lanette were spread, but that's inconsequential. He was probably out for another walk."

"Yeah." Jud jerked the blanket closed with his fist. "A walk."

"No, wait." Ryan pointed. "I remember seeing a truck in the alley. You couldn't have been walking. But you do admit you were there."

The corner of Katherine's lips twitched. Oh, her officemate was clever. She knew Ryan couldn't positively identify the vehicle.

But Jud didn't.

"Huh?" The wrinkles on Jud's forehead multiplied. "Yes, but, I mean I—"

"You admit it?"

"Admit what? That I tried to help my boy Harry with his campaign?" Jud's chin firmed. "Gladly. And I'd do it again."

"Jud," Mayor Johnson said. "You hung all those mean pictures of Lanette?"

He snickered. "Had a time finding any shots without her makeup on. But I made do. Since we've known each other so many years, I've still got enough unused material from camping trips and workdays to wallpaper the whole town."

"Let me at him!" Lanette vaulted around her husband, but Mayor Johnson grabbed her by the waist before she reached Jud.

Katherine's lips curled in disgust. "What about accusing Elise Walker of embezzlement? She might have gone to jail."

"Oh, please." He rolled his eyes. "I knew they couldn't prove it, but it made a good distraction." He waggled his brows at Mayor Johnson. "They lost a whole day of work, thanks to me."

"Jud," Mayor Johnson's face drooped, "how could you be so underhanded?"

"Aw, Harry," his mouth turned down, "all I did was hang a few lousy pictures and such."

Katherine's rage reached the boiling point. Her nostrils flared. Ryan took a menacing step forward. "It's the *and such* we need to address. The truck parked in the alley was the same kind that ran Katherine off the road."

Jud's gaze cut to the side. "I did no such thing. I don't know who it was, but it's not his fault if the woman can't drive."

"Is that why you didn't bother to stop and check on her?" Ryan advanced within a foot of the perpetrator. "She wound up with a bloody nose and a totaled car."

"What?" Mayor Johnson sank on the end of the stretcher. "I never heard about this. Katie, are you all right?"

"Yes." She shoved a finger at Jud. "No thanks to him."

"Oh, honey." Lanette hurried over and threw her arms around Katherine's neck. "Forgive me for roping you into this whole fiasco."

"Don't blame yourself." Katherine patted her back. "How were you supposed to know what a monster Jud is?"

"Monster?" Jud leaped from the stretcher, pitched his hat on the ground, and pushed Ryan away. "You're painting a slanderous picture of me. I could sue you for defamation."

"Try it." Ryan retrieved the hat and shoved it at Jud's chest. "I have a lawyer friend in New York who specializes in harassment cases. We have enough evidence from your admission to take you to court. Even if we don't win, it'll bury you in legal fees for the next five years."

Jud fumbled at the hat with twitchy fingers and crushed it on his head. "There's no call for bringing the law in between friends."

Katherine moved out of Lanette's embrace and looped an arm through Ryan's. If she hadn't already been in love, watching him jump to her defense would have cinched it. After a lifetime of taking care of herself, it was nice to see someone in her corner ready to fight for her.

Sheriff Garcia cleared his throat. "Jud, I think it fair to point out you've made some pretty incriminating admissions. It's my job to inform you of your right to remain silent." He jerked a thumb at his deputy. "I'll let Hank tell you the rest."

"Garcia," Jud groused, "you don't believe this smooth-talking, big-city con artist, do you?"

When the deputy took him by the arm, Jud resisted. "Wait! The town hall deal is still on. Right, Harry? You'll still buy my land?"

He whimpered as the deputy led him away.

The sheriff tipped his hat to Ryan. "Thanks for saving me hours of work. All of you come in later and give your statements. It can wait until we get a good night's sleep."

He nodded at everyone and walked away.

Mayor Johnson sat silent on the stretcher with Lanette at his side. She ignored the pathetic would-be saboteur. Her attention focused on her husband.

The mayor's chin almost touched the ground. He wore the expression of a man who'd lived a year full of Mondays. His eyes met Katherine's.

"Katie, words aren't enough," he whispered, "but I'm so sorry."

She let go of Ryan and crouched in front of the mayor. "There's no reason for you to be sorry. You had no idea Jud was doing such awful things."

Ryan drew closer. "He must have been worried he'd lose his payday if Lanette was elected."

Mayor Johnson shook his head. "I should have suspected—"

"Stop talking nonsense." Lanette slapped his back hard.

"Ow!" Mayor Johnson winced and rubbed the spot. "Darlin', that hurt."

"You deserved it." She pulled him to his feet. "I'm standing here at this unearthly hour without a stitch of makeup, and you're apologizing for something you didn't even do. I've suffered two nights on the rock-hard mattress in Elise's spare room, and I need to be in my own bed."

Katherine straightened and Ryan smiled at her. Leave it to Lanette to make a reconciliation sound like a fight.

"Does this mean you're coming home?" Harry's expression resembled a tired basset hound.

"Yes, honey." Lanette's face softened. "I'm coming home."

"Oh, thank God." Mayor Johnson wrapped her in a bear hug and lifted her feet off the ground.

"Harry Beauregard Johnson, put me down this instant." Her giggles belied her outraged tone.

Katherine looked at the starry night sky. Time to stop intruding on this private scene. Ryan must have had the same idea. He put his arm around her shoulders, and they snuck away together.

~

RYAN CUDDLED KATHERINE to his side as they wandered through the park, unhampered by the lack of light. Early morning mist stretched across the grass, and Katherine's soft body slumped against his. The ends of her ponytail brushed his wrist while they walked in weary contentment. They settled on a bench at the pond's edge, and Ryan kept his arm around her shoulders.

Peace drifted through the silence. If he were still a praying man, Ryan would be tempted to thank the good Lord it was over. He knew his emotions had nothing to do with the mayor's campaign. If word got out about Jud, it might be bad for the election. But the overwhelming relief of knowing Katherine was safe topped every concern.

She stirred beside him and released a breath. "I'm not surprised Jud was behind everything, but it's still sad for the mayor. They've been friends for decades. Thank you for tricking a confession out of him."

"Tricking?" Ryan glanced sideways at her.

"What word do you prefer? Finagling?"

"Forget it." He snorted and shifted on the bench. The quiet chirp of an insect sounded in the distance. "I guess I should thank you too."

"For what?" Her body turned his way.

He withdrew his arm and faced her. "Trusting me. You were ready to jump all over him, but you let me take the lead."

"It wasn't easy."

Her eyes sparkled in the pre-dawn light, and he smiled from somewhere deep inside. But as he turned away, the fear crept in.

He liked this feeling too much. What if he couldn't give it up when it was time to return to real life? Sweetheart was a charming dream destined to end. And the better the fantasy, the more bitter the wake-up. A twinge of panic hit, but he was distracted by the sweet pressure of Katherine's hand taking his.

No harm in enjoying the reverie a few seconds longer.

Tension hovered between them like the vibrations of a plucked guitar string. Ryan stared straight ahead. He quashed the rising emotions as her fingers laced with his. Their palms pressed together—a perfect fit.

She gave a soft laugh. "What a shame we didn't bring the sticky notes."

His finger tapped twice on the bench seat. Three times. Then Ryan turned, raised his free hand, and grasped behind her neck, pulling her in. His lips swooped down and covered hers. They moved against her full mouth with a gentle insistence.

Campaigns and strategies and future regrets flew from his mind. They'd danced around this moment for so long it seemed inevitable, but the press of her warm, supple lips on his was a hundred times sweeter than he'd imagined. His arms slipped around her waist and tugged her closer.

Katherine melted against him for the briefest of seconds before she pressed her fingers to his chest and pushed lightly.

With reluctance, he released her. His mind scrambled for the correct apology. She'd made her position clear, and he'd stepped over the line.

"I," Katherine gulped and smoothed her hair, "I don't want to stop kissing you, but we still have unresolved issues. Hopefully, we can continue this another time."

"Another time?" A belly laugh erupted from him.

She was incorrigible and utterly adorable.

How was he ever going to leave her?

Chapter
Twenty-Five

K atherine sat at Lanette's kitchen table with an overfilled mug of chamomile tea heating her fingers. Her heart begged to relive the kiss she'd shared with Ryan hours before, but her brain knew she had business with her employer, and she dreaded the conversation.

She spooned a generous dollop of honey in the tea and stirred. "How's the mayor?"

Lanette pulled a bottle of nail polish remover off the counter, opened the cap, and doused a cotton ball. "Not so great. One of his best friends sold his soul for money, and Harry blames himself." She settled in the chair next to her.

"He shouldn't." Katherine pounded the table, and tea sloshed from the rim of her mug.

Lanette reached to the wooden dispenser in the middle and passed her a napkin. "Harry feels responsible. Says if he hadn't agreed to buy Jud's land, none of this would've happened."

Katherine wiped the spilled tea and crumpled the wet paper. "Jud Watson made his own stupid choices."

"I agree. But my husband's a stubborn man who believes friendship is a serious business." Lanette dabbed at the white tips of her fingernails as the silence stretched. She released a stream of air from her nostrils and spoke. "It's time to take off our makeup and exit the stage, Katie."

Katherine clenched her mug. The hot ceramic burned her skin, and she let go. "What do you mean?"

"Harry's decided to cancel the fifteen million in bonds and use the old bank for a town hall." Her boss didn't look up. "So, I'm dropping out of the race."

Katherine clasped her hands in her lap. A lime green stain ran down one jean pant leg. It was left over from yesterday's brainstorming session when she'd been making an impassioned point about the town's pothole problem to Lanette with a highlighter. She'd planned to draw up a proposal for ways they could raise money without increasing taxes.

The research. The spreadsheets. The canvassing. That mountain of work had been for nothing. It was useless, but she refused to let it go easy.

"How can you quit? After all we've gone through?"

"I'm sorry, darlin'. It can't be helped."

Katherine searched the room as if she'd find a way to change Lanette's mind hiding in the corner pantry. "But ... but we're starting to make headway."

Lanette finished one hand and got to work on the other. "That's what changed my mind." She scrubbed at her nails with a concentrated vigor. "I was so bound and determined to keep Sweetheart out of the hole I didn't consider what losing the race would do to my husband." She dropped the cotton ball and met Katherine's eyes. "I love that man, Katie. He's naïve and gullible and spends way too much money on the latest gadgets, but he's got a good soul."

"The best." She rubbed a finger against the bridge of her nose. "But—"

"He's from the old school where the husband calls the shots. That's not really how it works in my family. We all know it. Including Harry. But having his wife publicly beat him out of a job he's held for sixteen years might crush him."

Katherine leaned over and grabbed Lanette's hand. Only two of the nails had any French tips left. Her brain careened through the list of arguments she could make.

"He loves you more than anything, Lanette. He'll forgive you."

"Oh, I know." She chuckled. "I've got him wrapped around my little unpolished finger." She waved her pinky in the air.

They laughed together at the truth of it.

Lanette laid her free hand on top of Katherine's. "You don't have much experience with matters of the heart, Katie, but I'll give you a tip. Sometimes love is letting the other person win, even if you hold every ace."

She shook her head. "You'd make a great mayor."

"I know," Lanette withdrew her fingers and retrieved the cotton ball, "but I'll make the sacrifice. It's not like Harry and I can both give up. One of us has to take care of Sweetheart."

Katherine slumped in her chair. Two months of backbreaking labor. Gone. She'd allowed herself to picture life after the campaign. Working with Lanette to better the town. What now?

Now she was an unemployed loser without a plan.

Again.

She tapped her hand against the table. What about the town council suggestion? She'd have to wait until the next election, but if she put her hard-won campaign knowledge to work, she might win a seat. Then she wouldn't have to push her ideas through someone else's platform.

Where was Ryan? He'd encouraged her to follow this political path. Perhaps he could help her strategize.

"You don't have to leave right away, son." Mayor Johnson loaded his fork with a heaping bite of chicken fried steak and swirled it in the milky-white gravy.

"I know, sir."

The corner booth Ryan had selected meant no other customers in The Brunch Café could overhear their discussion. He shifted against the shiny, red vinyl and straightened the cuff of his white shirt. He'd barely tasted his cup of plain black coffee.

Too many decisions to make. Avoiding Katherine hadn't been easy, but he needed space to think. Her stimulating presence short-circuited his brain.

"My wife told me she's dropping out of the race." The mayor talked around a mouthful of food. "I don't need a political consultant anymore, but I've grown kind of fond of you."

"Thank you." Ryan smiled. "I'm fond of you as well. But the sooner I return to my real life, the better. I've been away too long."

"It's a pity." Mayor Johnson set his fork down. "I kind of hoped you might stick around." He looked up with a puppy-dog expression. "I imagine Katherine Bruno feels the same way."

Ryan averted his gaze and took a long swig of the unsweetened brew in his mug.

"Sorry." The mayor scrunched his face. "It's not my place to pry. You two have to figure this out yourselves."

"There's nothing to figure out." He thunked his cup on the table. "She lives here. I live in New York. She likes adopting lost causes and talking to God out loud, and I like making money and living to please myself."

His dinner companion pushed his lips forward. "Doesn't resemble the person I've been campaigning with for the past couple months. The Ryan Park I know is a hard-working, honorable man who sacrifices his time to help others, regardless of what side of the aisle they're standing on. And I'm sure I didn't imagine the spark in your eye whenever Katie was near."

"I won't deny it. I admire her." Ryan pushed the salt and pepper shakers closer together. "Who wouldn't? She's beautiful. Clever. Creative. Funny—"

"I can see how you'd want to get away from that," the mayor deadpanned.

"But she bleeds Sweetheart." He raised his chin. "I'd have to give up everything for her. My home. My career. Everything I've worked for."

"Can't argue there." The mayor grabbed his fork and dug into the food. "Better to forget her and live your normal life."

"What?"

Wasn't the old man going to extol the virtues of sacrificing for love?

Mayor Johnson swallowed a giant bite of mashed potatoes. "I've known Katherine Bruno since she was a baby. She came out of the womb arguing, but it's always on the side of truth and justice. No one's been strong enough to match her. Not till now. You two make quite a team, but if you're not brave enough to take the risk," he waved his fork in the air, "best to leave her alone. She'll find someone better."

The vinyl booth creaked as Ryan sat back. Someone better?

It was true. His bitter, twisted, unforgiving soul didn't deserve Katherine. He was doing her a favor by leaving.

Chapter
Twenty-Six

C *lick. Click. Click. Click.*
Katherine's fingers flew across the laptop keys. Potholes weren't the only problem in Sweetheart. The animal shelter desperately needed a bigger building, and the elementary school could use a new playground.

She stretched her arms above her head. Other than taking the dogs for a quick run, she'd been at it all morning. Her list of proposed improvements already filled two pages.

She paused.

Running for town council was simpler than running for mayor. Was she spreading herself too thin? Should she build her campaign around one major issue?

Ryan would know. She had watched for him yesterday without success. Where was he?

Ding-dong.

Bella's joyous yips informed her who was outside.

"Co-ming," Katherine sing-songed. She skipped to the door and threw it open. "Where have you been? I need advice on—"

The words caught in her throat when she noted the wheeled suitcase at his side. His fingers rested on the extended handle like he was waiting for a plane.

Bella dashed around his ankles and pawed at his legs.

Ryan bent to pick her up. "I've come to say goodbye." He ran a gentle hand over the puppy's small head.

Katherine stared. "Goodbye as in I'm headed to the supermarket? Or goodbye as in forever?"

He shifted Bella under one arm and grasped the suitcase. "I'm booked on an evening flight to New York. I'll drive to Dallas and turn in my rental car."

She looked from the suitcase to him and back again. Placing a palm to her forehead, she stuttered, "I—I knew you planned to leave eventually, but I thought, I mean, I hoped—I'm surprised it's so soon. The election's tonight."

"It's a foregone conclusion. I admit I'm going to miss Sweetheart," he scratched the puppy behind her ears, "and this little imp. But my real life is in New York."

"Sweetheart's just a job to you?" A lava flood of hot emotion rose, and she was the volcano. She'd either scream or cry at any second. Neither was acceptable. Grabbing a bottle of water from the table by the door, she twisted off the cap and pressed it to her lips, more as a stopper than anything else.

God, I'm about to lose it here.

She gulped the cool liquid for an endless ten seconds. Must stay calm. Must not spew a fiery stream of words at Ryan.

He stood in the same spot as if he knew it wasn't over. By this time, she could read him in a heartbeat. His polite smile invited her to wrap up her spiel, so he could climb in his rental car and hit the road.

Katherine drew in enough air to extinguish fifty birthday candles and let it out in a noisy gust. "I thought you'd grown attached to our town. Become invested. Cared about its future."

"I care about a lot of things, but ..."

A thousand unspoken excuses filled Katherine's brain.

I was here temporarily.

New York offers more opportunities.

Did you really think I'd give up everything for Sweetheart? For you?

In the end, he didn't say any of them.

He stood with the unfinished excuse hanging. An impenetrable barrier. Glancing away, he shrugged.

Her heart deflated faster than a tire with a screw in it. Ryan had no desire to stay with her. She was like a foster dog. A cute distraction to fill a few lonely hours, but he'd ultimately given her back.

Her gaze dropped to somewhere around the second button of his perfectly ironed white shirt. "I see."

She spoke the words through clenched teeth. Any movement would unleash the tears, and she refused to be the weepy small-town girl he bragged about to his cosmopolitan buddies.

Calm.

Cool.

Crushed.

At least he'd never know the last part.

Ryan rubbed Bella's head before passing her over to Katherine. Their hands brushed, and she jerked away. The puppy whimpered and stretched her body at Ryan. His arms raised but dropped again.

Katherine petted the dog's head, avoiding eye contact. "You're not the type to quit before the job is done."

"My assignment was to make sure Harry Johnson was re-elected mayor. With no one running against him, I've accomplished my objective. His name is alone on the ballot."

Katherine's voice sounded foreign to her ears. As if someone else was talking. "I see your point. There's no reason for you to stay." She looked up. "Right?"

His eyes searched her face. He opened his mouth and stopped. Cleared his throat.

"Take care of yourself, Katherine." Ryan grabbed his suitcase. "Thanks for everything."

He walked down the porch steps. His luggage wheels

banged against the concrete as Bella barked and whined, but Katherine said nothing.

She went inside the house and shut the door with a soft click. No standing on the porch, watching him leave. Too pathetic. Romeo appeared from the other room to see what troubled his sister. Katherine set her on the floor, returned to the couch, and picked up her laptop.

An engine revved in the front yard. The faint sound of Ryan driving away stabbed her in the gut.

Her fingers rested on the keys for a long time. What did it matter anyway? No one would elect a hothead like her. Her best chance to make changes was through Lanette, who'd officially withdrawn her name from the ballot yesterday.

The story was over.

No happy ending.

A sour lump of emotion surged in Katherine's throat, and she swallowed it down. She swiped at tears. Crying fixed nothing. It wouldn't make Lanette reconsider. And it wouldn't bring Ryan back.

Regret hit so hard it stopped her breath. Her mind spun with the words she should have said. Instead of standing there with Bella making more fuss than she did. For a woman who'd spent a lifetime trying to control her tongue, she'd been remarkably silent.

Would he have stayed if she asked him? Or laughed in her face?

She'd never know.

He was gone.

Katherine shouted at the ceiling, "Why, God? Did you bring him here to taunt me with what I couldn't have?"

She grabbed a throw pillow and chucked it across the room. Romeo and Bella chased after it. Their noisy howls mirrored the pain in her soul. Despair whispered. What was left? Embrace the tidal wave of sorrow crashing over her? Climb into bed and stay there for a week?

As Katherine stood with computer in hand, she caught a glimpse of her reflection in a mirror hanging on the opposite wall. Her slumped image stared back—needy and miserable. She raised her chin.

No! Curling into a pitiful little ball was not an option. Being dumped was no excuse for quitting. There was too much to do. She may not have won Ryan's heart, but she could use what he'd taught her.

And cry later.

Katherine sat and tapped the mouse pad with a finger. The cursor blinked on her wish list of improvements for Sweetheart. She swiped one renegade tear from her eye and wiped her runny nose with her sleeve.

Later.

If she was going to be an old maid crusader, she was going to be the best one in the history of Sweetheart. No time to think about the shoulda-coulda-wouldas.

Chapter Twenty-Seven

Ryan drove along Main Street at a moderate speed. He passed the campaign office with hot pink-haired Lady Liberty on the outside and slowed to a snail's crawl. His gaze swerved from left to right, trying to memorize every detail of the picturesque town where he'd experienced such unexpected peace.

Flower boxes with a Lone Star on the front lined the sidewalk, overflowing with cheerful daisies. The large picture window of The Brunch Café showed customers crowded around the cozy tables. A truck meandered down the opposite side of the road. The driver tipped his cowboy hat as he passed.

Ryan waved. Friendly small-town manners. He'd never get used to them.

But he didn't have to. He was leaving.

It was the right decision, although everything inside of him disagreed. He refused to let emotions influence his choices. If he did, he would have never abandoned Katherine. Especially in the cruel, casual manner he'd chosen. How could she know it was killing him to drive away?

Part of Ryan had wished she'd throw another fiery fit and demand he reconsider, but she'd let him go without a fight.

A host of reasons to turn around crowded his brain, but she was the only one that mattered. Not that he would tell her. He needed to leave while he still could. Before he chucked his pride, his career, and his entire future out the window.

His foot pressed the accelerator. Sweetheart sped by until it was a speck in his rearview mirror. He drove along the feeder road and took a left onto the interstate.

Time to head home to ... to what?

A harried, stress-filled lifestyle, catering to self-absorbed politicians who broke their promises the moment it became inconvenient. Even the good ones chose compromise over failure. Why was he in such a hurry to rejoin the cesspool?

Ryan ground his teeth. He'd grown soft in Sweetheart.

The easy pace. The caring citizens. Katherine.

They'd surprised him like a gift from above.

His foot slipped off the gas. Where did that idea come from?

Was Katherine right? Had he blamed God for everything that went wrong while giving Him no credit for the good things? Ryan spent many years denying the existence of a loving Heavenly Father, but how else could he explain the last few months?

How did a lifelong die-hard New Yorker find himself in the smallest corner of Texas if not by divine intervention? Was it just a coincidence he'd worked in the same office and lived next door to the only woman who'd ever touched his soul?

A deafening honk sounded behind him. He swerved. A semi cut around and sped away with another angry blare of its horn. Ryan clocked his speedometer. Going thirty-five miles an hour on an interstate highway was asking for trouble. He accelerated, but his mind refused to shut the door his mutinous thoughts had snuck open.

His heart pounded faster than his engine. He opened his mouth to speak.

One time.

Twice.

"God?" he whispered.

It was a far cry from Katherine's unashamed declarations.

"God?" He spoke a little louder. "Are You there?"

The noisy buzz of the car speeding over the concrete answered.

What was he doing? If there was an Almighty God listening, why would He acknowledge a sinner like him?

Ryan rolled his shoulders. He should concentrate on driving. Focusing on the road ahead, his eyes caught a glimmer to his right. An iridescent, almost invisible rainbow stretched above a thick patch of oak trees.

Strange.

He hadn't noticed any rain.

God keeps his promises.

Ryan heard his mother's voice as if she were sitting in the passenger seat beside him.

It was her favorite saying, each time she spotted a rainbow. He must have heard it a thousand times growing up. He and his sister used to quote it with her in teasing high-pitched tones.

Ryan released a ragged gasp. The tears flooded his vision. He scrubbed them away.

Like Noah of old, his world was destroyed by a flood of grief and bitterness. It blotted out the sun and made the best of times barely tolerable. But when he'd come to Sweetheart, the waters receded. He'd thrown open the window to his soul and breathed the fresh air once again.

"Did You do that, God?" he croaked.

The baseball-sized lump in his throat blocked the words.

Ryan pulled over to the side of the road. The huge Texas sky stretched above him in a sunny, blue blanket. White, wispy clouds swirled across the enormous expanse. He stared at the rainbow in the distance. The colors beckoned him with an invitation of hope.

Time to put away the pain of the past.

Time to build a new life.

He gripped the steering wheel and rested his forehead against it. Scenes from the past two months rolled through his mind. A living testimony of goodness and mercy.

"God," Ryan raised his head and laughed, "if You truly brought Katherine into my life then she was right. I am a fool. 'Cause I'm driving in the wrong direction."

He put the car in gear and sped to the nearest exit. Would she forgive him? He'd only been gone thirty minutes. But after his off-handed goodbye speech, he had fences to mend.

Ryan exited in a town even smaller than Sweetheart, drove under the overpass, and stopped at a traffic light. He drummed his fingers against the wheel, anxious to return before she cranked her temper to nuclear levels.

She still loved him. That he didn't doubt. His hard-headed Katherine never gave up on something once she began. It was a shame she hadn't run for mayor.

Ryan's fingers stilled. The light changed, and he turned left, merging onto the interstate, heading to Sweetheart. His mind whirled as he drove. Why was he thinking of the election? It was over. His candidate would win in a landslide.

But Harry Johnson didn't want to be mayor. Was he crazy to consider this? The rainbow glowed from his left as he passed, and Ryan laughed out loud.

"Wow, God. You're not taking it easy on me, are You?"

Chapter Twenty-Eight

K atherine dragged her feet into the community center ten minutes before voting closed. The room's dark wood paneling matched her mood. She cast a baleful glance at the two curtained booths at the side. Time to do her duty.

What was the point? There was one name on the ballot.

Harry Beauregard Johnson.

He was a good mayor and a good man, but her spirit rebelled. After devoting a summer of sweat and tears to campaigning with his wife, Katherine couldn't do it. She'd write in Lanette Johnson's name, whether the woman was an official candidate or not. She owed her that much.

Katherine pulled a rubber band from her purse and tied up her hair before signing in with the clerk. She took a ballot, slipped into the curtained booth, and scribbled Lanette's name into the alternate blank at the bottom.

What if there were others like her? The debate may have changed a few minds. Miracles still happened. Her lips quirked as she wrote. She always did favor impossible causes.

Katherine slipped the folded paper in the box, withdrew the curtain, and froze.

Ryan stood across the room, dressed in a tailored navy suit

with a white dress shirt and red tie, talking to the minister's wife. Mary Thibodeaux nodded and pointed at a group of Ladies Auxiliary members sitting near the stage. He bent his head in concentration, unaware her shattered heart was a few yards away.

What was he doing here?

Had Mayor Johnson asked him to stay until the election was officially over?

Or did Ryan change his mind?

She grasped the curtain, the material clenched in her fist. Had he found it impossible to leave Sweetheart? To leave her?

Their eyes met.

Her body swayed forward.

And Ryan walked away. He headed for the group of women Mary had indicated, approached with his most charming smile, and shook each of their hands.

Katherine stepped back into the booth and yanked the curtain closed.

Idiot.

She meant nothing to him. Hadn't he already proven it the first time he left? He was just wrapping up loose ends. Doing what he did best. Making people dance to his tune.

She leaned her head against the side of the booth.

"God, I'm all out of gracious words." She bonked her skull against the frame. "Help me not to be an embarrassment to You or myself."

"Are you done, Katie?" A voice called from outside.

Katherine pressed her fists against her temples. She would get through this. It was that or hide in here for the rest of her life.

She eased the curtain back. It was better than ripping it from the rod and hiding under the heavy fabric. She exited the booth and jerked her head for the next person to enter.

Katherine chose a seat in the last row. Might as well wait. They'd announce the winner soon. She studied Ryan as he canvassed every woman in the room.

Except for her, of course. He never even looked her way.

Was the AC broken? The suffocating lack of air made her break into a sweat. Katherine fanned herself. Hold it together. Spine straight, she crossed her legs and wrapped her hands around her knees.

"What's wrong?" Deanna plopped in the chair beside Katherine, her violet poodle skirt poofing around her. "You're sitting like someone enrolled you in an etiquette class."

Katherine pressed her lips together in the closest thing to a smile she could muster. "What do you mean? I'm fine."

"Uh-huh." Deanna gave her a sidelong look and made air quotes with her fingers. "Fine."

Katherine angled her body away, hoping Deanna would take the hint. She spent a few minutes in silent reflection. Her brain sharpened the harsh words she wanted to say to Ryan. Then she asked God for forgiveness. She thought of another insult to hurl in that egotistical know-it-all's face. Then she asked for forgiveness again. It was an endless cycle.

Deanna poked her. "They're finished counting. Time for the results."

Katherine took one last fortifying breath. She surveyed the room and found Ryan standing by the wall near the platform. His stance was tense. Alert. Not quite as assured as usual. They made eye contact, and she ducked her head.

Pastor Thibodeaux stood on the stage with the microphone and a sheet of paper. "The votes have been tallied." He cocked his chin to the side and paused. "Before I read this, let me remind everyone the Lord moves in mysterious ways."

Katherine locked her molars together. She was not in the mood for a sermon, but it wouldn't do to holler at the minister.

He flapped the piece of paper in his hand. "I believe He's orchestrated everything once again for His good and perfect will. I hope the citizens of Sweetheart will support the winner, regardless of who they voted for."

She couldn't take anymore. Katherine unzipped her gray

purse and pushed through the jumble to the side pocket. She remembered putting a mini candy bar in there a few days ago.

Pastor Thibodeaux put on his reading glasses and cleared his throat. "Harry Johnson received one hundred fifty-two votes."

Katherine's head jerked up. That was way less than expected. She'd heard a lot of citizens weren't bothering to vote once Mayor Johnson was the lone candidate. Had it affected the outcome? Did anyone else write in Lanette's name?

The pastor lifted a finger off the microphone to push his glasses further up the bridge of his nose. "Nine write-in votes went to Lanette Johnson."

Her hopes wilted. When would she ever learn? No matter how hard she worked, things never changed. What was the point of trying? A familiar crinkle hit her fingers, and she pulled out the tiny candy bar. Katherine ripped off the wrapper, shoved the entire chocolate in her mouth, and sighed.

"And the winner with one hundred fifty-six write-in votes, the newly elected mayor of Sweetheart is," Pastor Thibodeaux scanned the audience as if enjoying the drama, "Katherine Bruno."

Katherine choked on a peanut. He'd said her name. There must be some mistake.

People cheered. Others gasped and looked her way with horror.

The chocolate melted in a sweet glob on her tongue, but she didn't have the strength to swallow. Her gaze flashed to Ryan.

He'd relaxed against the wall. His peaceful expression betrayed no surprise. His eyes cut over to her, and he grinned.

Had he known about this?

Deanna hopped up beside her and clapped. "Woo-hoo, Katherine. Speech! Speech!"

Katherine yanked her friend down by her poofy skirt. This must be a dream. Or a nightmare. Her brain stalled like it was swimming in fondue, unable to hold one coherent thought.

Harry and Lanette ascended the steps.

Mayor Johnson took the microphone from the minister. "My fellow citizens, in case anyone is wondering, this is all legal. The great state of Texas allows write-in candidates, and I fully support the practice. I've craved retirement for years. I'm certain Katherine loves this town with her whole heart and will offer her unflagging devotion to make sure no one takes advantage of it. Before we let our new mayor give her acceptance speech, there's a young man who has asked to say a few words."

Ryan climbed the stairs to the stage. His glossy black hair spilled onto his forehead. Pushing it back, he unbuttoned his suit jacket and took the mic from Harry Johnson. "Ladies and gentlemen, I have a confession to make."

Deanna gave a tiny squeal and whispered, "A confession. Maybe he's going to propose."

"Don't be ridiculous," Katherine ground out. A few hours ago, he'd driven away without a second glance. She didn't know why he was here, but it wasn't for romance.

Ryan motioned to Pastor Thibodeaux, standing at the side of the platform. "I'm not a citizen of Sweetheart—yet."

Katherine held her breath.

"But, if I had a vote, I would have cast it for your new mayor. Katherine Bruno and I represented opposing sides in this election, and you've probably heard her get upset with me on more than one occasion."

A wave of laughter passed through the audience. Even Pastor Thibodeaux slapped his knee. But Katherine wasn't enjoying the joke. She smoothed the collar of her T-shirt.

Ryan moved around the lectern and walked to the edge of the stage. "I've worked in close proximity to Ms. Bruno for months, and I'll testify in court there isn't a stronger, smarter, more hardworking woman in the whole country."

"Awwwww," Deanna whimpered as she wiggled in her seat.

Katherine bit the inside of her lower lip. She had no idea what Ryan was building up to, but she didn't want to miss a word.

"She blazes through every day as if she truly believes she can make a difference," he looked straight at her, "and she got a hard-bitten cynic like me believing it. Believing in a lot of things —good people, destiny, God."

She was going to lose it in front of her neighbors. Katherine swiped a quick hand under each eye and sucked in a lungful of air. Ryan took no mercy on her embarrassing predicament and continued.

"Because of her, I've reconnected with my faith and my desire to do something good for the world. I encourage everyone who didn't vote for Katherine to give her the chance to prove herself, because she will." He smiled. "Over and over. Until the rest of us are left exhausted at her unending passion for Sweetheart."

"Amen!" Mary Thibodeaux called from the front row.

Deanna jumped to her feet again and applauded.

Lanette beckoned from the stage for Katherine to join them.

Her husband grabbed the microphone from Ryan. "Mayor Bruno, please come here and let me be the first to congratulate you."

Katherine's body raised from the chair like it was a puppet on strings. Her feet propelled her down the aisle, but she had no clue how they were moving. If she was the mayor, she could initiate her plan to turn the bank into a town hall. She could allocate funds to the animal shelter for expansion. She could develop a program to lease empty city buildings on Main Street to young entrepreneurs for a set percentage of their profit. She could—

Her head swam with the possibilities. She needed her laptop.

"Katherine?"

She realized she'd stopped at the edge of the platform. Ryan stood at her side. He held out a hand, ready to help her onto the stage. His lopsided smirk reassured her. She grasped the strong fingers and stepped up—into a whole new world of only God knew what. She trembled as she walked to the podium.

What should a newly elected mayor say first?

She adjusted the microphone in its holder and cleared her throat. "I bet a lot of you didn't vote for me."

Not the most eloquent start, but it was truthful. Many faces stared at her with a mixture of surprise and dismay.

"If you didn't, I don't blame you. I'm headstrong and opinionated and hard to get along with, but I love this town. I fight so hard because I want the best for Sweetheart. For all of us." She stretched an open palm at the crowd and paused. "I admit it. I have zero experience and a big mouth."

Katherine looked over at Ryan. He sighed and shook his head.

Her smile threatened to stretch to her ears. "But give me a chance. Please. I'll win you over by sheer grit and determination."

She finished her speech and stepped off the stage. The Ladies Auxiliary attacked her en masse. Each required a hug and a personal thank you for their contribution to her success. Other citizens whispered a kind word, but many rushed out the door with cell phones pressed to their ears—anxious to tell the rest of the town what they'd missed.

Katherine endured the back slapping and good-natured congratulations while she counted the seconds until she could talk to the man who mattered most. He waited patiently near the exit until the crowd dispersed.

Katherine hurried down the middle aisle, running her fingers over the top of her hair.

Oops.

She was wearing a messy ponytail again. She'd planned to vote and run. Not win an election.

She stopped in front of Ryan. "How did you make this happen?"

He shrugged. "Mayor Johnson already confided in me he was ready to retire if someone worthy would take his place. Then I had a flash of inspiration."

"Or insanity."

He raised a brow. "I shared my opinion with Mayor Johnson that you'd make a great replacement. He passed it on to Lanette who gathered her Ladies Auxiliary cronies and a few other friends."

Swish. Swish. Swish.

Except for one lone custodian sweeping the stage, they were the only people in the room.

Katherine scratched the side of her head. Could she do this?

Absolutely.

Because she had to. She'd been elected mayor, and backing down from a challenge was inconceivable.

She studied her greatest challenge as he stood before her. "This morning, you were driving away with your suitcase packed. What changed your mind?"

Ryan shoved his hands in his pockets. "God and I had a little talk."

Katherine grasped him by the elbows. "Did you two make up?"

The corner of his mouth twitched. "I'd say we're getting there."

Forget being elected mayor. This was the best news of the evening. Tears rushed to the surface. Her face crumpled, and a sob escaped.

"Whoa." Ryan withdrew his hands. "No need to cry about it."

He cupped her cheeks and swiped at the moisture with his thumbs. Katherine leaned her head against his chest and wrapped her arms around his waist.

The old, familiar doubt whispered in her brain. What if she failed?

A relationship.

Running the town.

Her inexperience with both terrified her.

Ryan smoothed her hair. "Don't start worrying about the details. Let yourself enjoy the moment."

She smiled at him. "Are you reading my mind?"

"Not yet," he flashed his eyebrows, "but I'm starting to figure out the way you think. And I'll get better with practice."

Someone who understood her and still wanted to stick around. Could there be anything sweeter?

She tamped down a new wave of tears. "But I don't know anything about being mayor."

He brushed a strand of hair from her face. "You'll learn."

"Can you recommend a good consultant to give me a few pointers?" She gazed into his dark sparkling eyes.

"There may be a certain New Yorker. His doctor told him to lower his blood pressure, and he might be willing to relocate to Sweetheart. For health reasons."

"Does he mind working for a woman?"

Ryan's electrifying grin appeared. "What do you take him for, an addlepated sexist?"

"I'm afraid the job doesn't pay much."

He pulled her closer. "I'm sure there are other perks that will make up for it. Let's say at least two date nights a week?"

"Sounds good to me." She leaned in and proceeded to take Ryan's advice and enjoy it.

She raised on her tiptoes and pressed her mouth to his lips. His hands settled against the small of her back, aligning her body to his.

There would be plenty to worry about later. Right now, she'd appreciate the gifts God had sent her way. She'd lived in Sweetheart her entire life, but she'd never experienced this level of belonging.

In Ryan's arms.

A sense of rightness overwhelmed her, and she whispered a quiet prayer of gratitude.

It was good to be home.

Epilogue

One year later
"Howdy, Mayor Bruno."

"Hello, Mr. Torres." Katherine waved her head at the older man as she climbed from her sedan. Bags, a drink carrier, and take-out containers filled her arms, and she pushed the car door shut with her hip. Even after all this time, she still wasn't used to her official title.

Katherine tottered to the office and kicked at the entrance, but no one answered. She lifted a finger from one of the bags, pried the door open, and shoved her elbow inside. The carrier in her other hand tilted at a precarious angle. She careened into the office, sloshing renegade drops of soda onto the tile floor.

"Hey. Can't you help a girl out?"

Ryan glared at her from his desk. He'd replaced the rickety broken-down one with a modern black-and-aluminum version. He jerked his chin to the side and nodded at the laptop in front of him. A young, squeaky voice from the screen nervously expounded on the benefits of perception analyzers in an election race.

Sorry, Katherine mouthed.

She tiptoed across the room to her own rosebud covered

escritoire. Good thing Lanette had let her keep it until the new town hall was ready. Sweetheart owned the old bank, but they still needed two hundred and forty thousand dollars to update the plumbing, rewire the electric, and buy furniture.

An urge to panic tempted her, but she suppressed it. Two hundred and forty thousand dollars was way better than fifteen million. At least she got to share office space with her gorgeous boyfriend while they raised funds for the renovations. Ryan had taken a position as an online professor for the college where his sister worked. He spent his days doing internet classes, political consultations, and helping her with Sweetheart stuff on the side.

Things were going well. Most of the townspeople had accepted or at least resigned themselves to her tenure as mayor. She dumped the food on her desk and turned. Ryan pointed an index finger to the right, his eyes never leaving the computer screen.

Katherine's gaze followed his gesture to find a giant yellow heart made of sticky notes on the far wall near the coffee-maker. She pressed her lips together. Must remain calm. It wouldn't be dignified for the mayor of Sweetheart to whoop like a high schooler.

She walked slightly faster than normal to examine the heart. As she drew closer, she observed a copier-sized sheet of paper on the side with an arrow pointing at the notes. Three words were handwritten in a neat, masculine scrawl.

Katherine Bruno is:

She peered at the heart. Each yellow sticky note held a different description.

Caring.

Tireless.

Gutsy.

A good ping-pong player.

She raised on her toes to see the notes at the top. They covered everything from her being a passionate crusader to the most beautiful ponytail-wearer in the world.

A squeak escaped her lips. She really couldn't help it. If he wanted his online classes to remain professional, he shouldn't create such cheesy, wonderful surprises. She whipped around.

How could he sit there as if he hadn't spun her insides like a carousel?

Ryan focused straight ahead.

"Excuse me, Professor." A tinny voice from the computer spoke. "When is our paper due?"

Ryan answered a few questions, wrapped up the class, and signed off. He rose and headed for her desk. "What took you so long? I'm starving."

Katherine inclined her head to the heart. "You put the time to good use."

Ignoring her comment, he unwrapped his burger and took a bite.

Okay. He wanted to play it cool.

She joined him at the desk and took a sip from her drink. "Sorry I interrupted your class."

He popped a crinkle fry in his mouth. "My sister was beyond grateful I agreed to teach the online Political Science courses at her college. She won't complain. Especially since she also roped me into covering Economics."

"Maybe you'd prefer Romantic Poetry." Katherine widened her eyes at the heart again.

His lips quirked. "What do you think?"

She wagged her head back and forth. "Not bad."

"What?" He crushed the wrapper around his burger and plopped it on the desk. "I expected a bigger reaction."

She threw her arms around his neck and planted a noisy kiss on his cheek. "I admit it. I love it."

"No." He pushed her away. "You said it was not bad. I must have missed something."

He swiped his sandwich and motioned to her desk. "Would you please clean this up? It's impossible to find anything."

Her brows lowered. She and Ryan had an occasional

disagreement like any normal couple—usually started by her—but how had this sweet, romantic moment turned into a fight?

She stuck her cup in the drink carrier and chucked it in the trashcan. As she moved to grab the takeout bag, a flash of yellow on the desk caught her attention. She pushed the bag aside and found one more sticky note. She lifted it to read:

Katherine Bruno is Heaven's best gift.

I love you.

Marry me.

A copper-colored key was taped to the bottom.

She pressed a palm to her mouth, the note wrinkling in her fingers.

Ryan put his arms around her. "Wow. I can count on one hand the number of times I've seen you cry. I hope those are happy tears."

Katherine nodded—unable to answer with words. After so many years of lonely singlehood, she'd doubted this day would ever come. A whirlpool of emotions churned inside of her: Relief, Excitement, Anticipation, Gratitude. The most overwhelming feeling was a knock-the-earth-out-from-under-her love for Ryan.

He nudged her closer. "I know I'm supposed to get down on one knee, but this way was more fitting for us. Do you mind?"

She shook her head.

Ryan laughed. "I should call Abe Kaiser at the newspaper. This may be the first time Katherine Bruno is speechless."

She eyed the crumpled note and studied the key. "I don't have much experience with engagements, but I thought guys normally proposed with a ring."

He shrugged. "After I bought the house on Quincy Street, there wasn't much money left over for diamonds.

"You bought my dream house?" She squealed. "How did you know?"

"You're kidding, right?" He scoffed. "You've only walked me by the place twenty times since I moved here. And each time, you mentioned how you'd live in it someday. If you want the dream to happen, you'll have to take me with the package. We'll say our vows, settle down, and fill our tiny kitchen with the scent of fresh-baked peppermint chocolate."

She stared at the yellow paper. "Do you mean it?"

"One hundred percent. We'll make beautiful cookies together."

"Not that." She swatted his chest. "The part in the note about me being your best gift."

Ryan nodded. "I can't believe God saved a woman as amazing as you for a hard-hearted wretch like me. But I'll spend the rest of my life being thankful."

"That makes two of us." She curled her fingers around the beautiful key. "Let's ask your father to perform the ceremony."

"I called him last night." Ryan gave her a smug smile. "He and my sister are booking airline tickets for February."

"February!" Katherine tried to pull away, but Ryan's hands kept her firmly in place against him. "So soon? Can we get everything done in time? We have to reserve the church, pick a honeymoon spot, find a dog sitter. And it has to be after the Candy Hearts Festival. It's the town's biggest event, and the mayor should be there. We—"

Ryan's head descended, and his mouth found hers. Schedules and to-do lists faded from Katherine's brain as she snuggled her newly engaged body against his. It had taken a long time for God to send the man to match her fiery personality, but every second of waiting was worth it in the end.

DISCUSSION QUESTIONS

1. Katherine Bruno is a fiery crusader who struggles to find the right outlet for her passion in small-town Sweetheart. Have you ever felt you didn't fit in? How did you find ways to connect with others?
2. Ryan Park works in the political arena and keeps a tight rein on his tongue. He rarely says what he truly thinks. Are you a person who keeps your opinions to yourself or someone who lays all their cards on the table? What are the positives and negatives of both approaches?
3. Lanette Johnson decides to run against her own husband for mayor and finds a willing group of supporters in the Ladies Auxiliary. Do you have a group of friends you can count on, no matter how whacky the situation gets? What is one crazy experience you and your friends went through together?
4. When Ryan failed to tell Katherine of a necessary form her campaign needed to file before the deadline, she was furious and blamed him. Do you feel he was dishonest or just a smart businessman? How might their relationship have changed if he had alerted her to the missing paperwork?
5. Katherine ropes Ryan into watching her foster dogs, even though he is an unwilling sitter, and the adorable puppies win over his jaded heart. Have you ever been given an unexpected pet that grew on you? What was the sweetest or funniest thing about them?
6. Despite being political rivals, Katherine's heart softens when Ryan takes care of her while she's sick. Was there ever a time you misjudged a person but later

became friends? Did the person change, or just your perception of them?

7. Never shy about sharing her emotions, Katherine confesses her feelings to Ryan when she realizes she likes him. Have you ever been the first to confess to someone you fancied? What was their response?

8. When Ryan comes upon Katherine after her car accident, the two have a heart-to-heart as they wait for the tow truck, and Katherine reveals her fruitless search to find the right career. Do you see your work as a paycheck or a calling? What are some ways God could use you at your job?

9. The unexpected death of his mother due to medical negligence left Ryan bitter. He blamed God for not stepping in and preventing the accident. Have you ever gone through a hard time when God felt far away? How did you hold on to your faith?

10. When Ryan leaves town, the zealous Katherine lets him go without a battle. Why didn't she fight for him to stay? Do you agree with the way she handled the situation?

11. It's been many long years of bitterness for Ryan, but he's finally able to let go when he's reminded of his mother's words—God keeps His promises—and realizes how many ways God has watched over him. What promises has God made to you? Have they all been fulfilled, or are you still trusting Him that some will happen?

12. Katherine is shocked to find herself elected the new mayor of Sweetheart. Has life ever surprised you with an unsought job or promotion? Did it scare or excite you? How did you handle the transition?

Acknowledgments

I did an interview where the person asked if family or friends had opposed my writing dream. The question stumped me. I couldn't think of a single instance. I've been blessed with a loving, supportive group of people who never once ridiculed my desire to create stories.

The greatest cheerleaders are my parents. Out of all the people in the world, I wonder how I ended up so blessed to be the daughter of Jim and Billie Sue Dunlap.

Another important team of encouragers is my Scribes 236 crew. Thank you for all your help honing and shaping this novel.

Lone Star Sweetheart might not be here now if it weren't for two very generous and talented writer friends, Janice Thompson and Kathleen Y'Barbo Turner. They opened the door for this book and helped me walk through it. Love y'all!

Thank you to Linda Fulkerson and Scrivenings Press for taking a chance on me! Your acceptance meant so much.

To all the people who appreciate my stories, you make it all worthwhile. When I read your comments about how a character made you laugh out loud, it's like a love letter straight to my heart. Your time is precious. Thank you for spending part of it with me and the hilarious citizens of Sweetheart!

God keeps his promises. I'm living proof of that. I thank Him for allowing me to grow up in His house, for leading me to the writing path, and holding my hand when I felt lost. I look forward in anticipation to see what He has next on the journey.

Shannon Sue Dunlap completed an M.A. in Journalism from Regent University in Virginia Beach, VA. She has sold and/or published articles with *Seek*, *The Secret Place*, *The Young Salvationist*, The Lorenz Corporation, and various e-magazines. Shannon spent three years as a contributing writer for a Virginia paper, Portfolio Weekly. She has also indie published a clean-and-wholesome romance novella and sequel novel (*Flower Boy Tour Guide* and *Reality Show Romance*) and a Christian romantic suspense (*Decoy Valentine*).

Shannon loves traveling and draws from her many experiences around the world. From New York City and Seoul, South Korea, to Gaborone, Botswana, these beautiful places have provided inspiration for her stories. When at home in Houston, Texas, she teaches music to an adorable bunch of students at a local school and writes in her free time. You can sign up for her newsletter at shannonsuedunlap.com.

You may also like ...

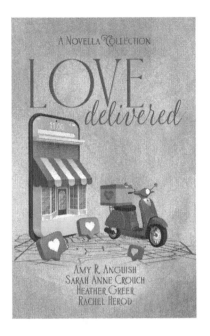

Love Delivered

A novella collection

Romance at Register Five (by Amy R Anguish)—Mack McDonald isn't happy about the Grocerease app coming to his grocery store. But he's committed to the sixty-day trial period, and braces himself to lose money. Kaitlyn Daniels loves how the Grocerease app helps her make ends meet so she can assist her mom, the reason she moved to small Sassafras, AR. Mack and Kaitlyn struggle to overcome differing opinions on the perks of the app. But if they don't, it could keep them from something even better.

Where Love is Planted (by Sarah Anne Crouch)—Ivy Aaronson is surrounded by family at their flower shop in West Texas—just the way she likes it. But she's given up hope on ever finding a man who understands her choices. When attorney Grant Keller orders flowers for his mother, Ivy wonders if maybe there are indeed some considerate men left in the world…until she finds out Grant's relationship with his parents is less than ideal. How can Ivy ever find love when every man she meets puts career over family?

Sweet Delivery **(by Heather Greer)**—After winning Cake That, Will Forrester thinks his Pastry Perfect Baking Dreams have come true. The sweetness fades when a chain bakery moves to town, and Will must adjust his plans to keep his customers. Hiring Erica Gerard is one of those changes. As they work together, Erica challenges Will and offers new ideas to improve the bakery. Soon, Erica and Will start bringing out the best in each other. But Erica harbors a secret, and if it's discovered, Will might never be the same.

The Mermaids, the Ex, and USSS **(by Rachel Herod)**—Braig Sanborn is the most loyal employee the United States Shipping Service has ever seen, which is why he agreed to transfer across the country with only a few weeks' notice. Bailey Bivens is so busy planning a friend's wedding, she didn't expect to fall for the carrier who delivers packages to her house. When they both find themselves in too deep, will they agree the relationship was doomed from the start?

Get your copy here:

https://scrivenings.link/lovedelivered

❦

Cake That!

Third-place Winner—Contemporary Romance

2022 Selah Awards

Ten bakers. Nine days. One winner.

Competing on the *Cake That* baking show is a dream come true for
Livvy Miller, but debt on her cupcake truck and an expensive repair
make her question if it's one she should chase. Her best friend, Tabitha,
encourages Livvy to trust God to care for The Sugar Cube, win or lose.

Family is everything to Evan Jones. His parents always gave up their
dreams so their children could achieve theirs. Winning *Cake That* would
let him give back some of what they've sacrificed by allowing him to
give them the trip they've always talked about but could never afford.

As the contestants live and bake together, more than the competition
heats up. Livvy and Evan have a spark from the start, but they're in it to
win. Neither needs the distraction of romance. Unwanted attention
from Will, another competitor, complicates matters. Stir in strange

occurrences to the daily baking assignments, and everyone wonders if a saboteur is in the mix.

With the distractions inside and outside the *Cake That* kitchen, will Livvy or Evan rise above the rest and claim the prize? Or does God have more in store for them than they first imagined?

Get your copy here:

scrivenings.link/cakethat

~

Destination: ~~Fun~~ Romance

Roadtrip Romance—Book One

It's not every day you bring a boyfriend back as a souvenir.

Katie Wilhite is ready to settle into her new job as a librarian now that college is through, but friends Bree and Skye want one more girls' trip, and when Bree insists this is her bachelorette fling, Katie agrees. What she didn't agree to was allowing fun and flighty Skye to dictate the itinerary or for her anxiety to kick in harder than ever ... right in front of a cute guy.

Camden Malone had no idea when he agreed to be the voice of reason on his cousin Ryan's vacation that the trip wouldn't stay in New Orleans as planned. But when Ryan plots with Skye so that the guys can tag along with the girls all week, he isn't nearly as upset as he should be. Not with Katie's fiery temper and flashing eyes intriguing him more by the minute.

Can Katie relax enough to trust Camden and a possible future, or will she continue to push him away as only a vacation fling? And can Camden move past a rocky history of his own to be able to jump into a better future? For a trip that was supposed to be all about fun, there's a lot of romance going around.

Get your copy here:

https://scrivenings.link/destinationromance

Scrivenings
PRESS
Quench your thirst for story.
www.ScriveningsPress.com

Stay up-to-date on your favorite books and authors with our free e-newsletters.

ScriveningsPress.com

Made in the USA
Coppell, TX
03 November 2023

23769952R00142